A Pursued Heart

Elaine Manders

Scripture references are taken from the New King James Version (NKJV) of the Bible.

Cover Design: Virginia McKevitt

Also special thanks to Lisa Prysock and all my fellow authors in the *Georgia Peaches Series* for their encouragement and contribution to this series.

May every reader be blessed and the Lord be magnified.

A Pursued Heart

Georgia Peaches

Message to Readers

Dear Reader

Thank you for buying my books, reading them, and supporting Christian fiction—even if you just like a clean romance. Your cards, letters, emails, and reviews lift my spirit and motivate me to write the next book.

If you would like to join the team to support this series, here is the link.

https://www.facebook.com/groups/877959952547231/

To get first-hand information about upcoming releases, have input to new books, join our parties for prizes and fun, and meet the authors. Subscribe to my newsletter at https://dl.bookfunnel.com/or10xrsvje, and receive a free novella.

It's better to light one small candle than to curse the darkness. I believe the Lord will bless our efforts to improve the culture through literature, even in this small way.

Be sure to check out all of my books.

https://www.amazon.com/Elaine-Manders/e/B0116MKKJG/ref=sr_tc_2_0?qid=1524173840&sr=1-2-ent

Prologue

It is not for you to know times or seasons which the Father put in His own authority. -Acts 1:7

One of God's greatest blessings is to shield us from seeing the future. I've loved two women in my life. If I had trusted my foresight, I might have saved the first one's life. Only by trusting God can I save the other one. – Benjamin Lucas

Steam fogged Ben Lucas's bathroom, and he adjusted the shower temperature. Just enough time to shower and shave before Kelly arrived. He'd reached around to pull his sweaty tee over his head when the doorbell rang.

Muttering, he tugged the shirt down and jerked the shower lever off, then rushed down the hall. Whoever it was had better be quick. He never got unexpected visitors out here on the sleepy side of town, and he liked it that way.

It wasn't really hot enough to work up a sweat. In fact, barely a week had passed since the last of the snow had melted, but Ben wanted the yard to be perfect. He and Kelly were getting married back there.

Ready to send the salesman on his way, he slammed the door open. Kelly stood on the stoop, her young son, Jamie, beside her. His irritation melted faster than the remaining snow. He didn't even think to be surprised.

He pulled her across the threshold and into his arms, breathing in the familiar fragrance of her trendy, department store cologne. Somewhere in the haze of his brain he imagined what he must smell like, having just mowed the lawn. But she didn't seem to mind as they kissed long and deeply.

"Yuk!"

Jamie's high-pitched opinion pulled then apart, laughing. "Better get used to it, buddy, your mom and I are getting married next Saturday."

Hands on Kelly's shoulders, Ben held her at arm's length and gazed into her beautiful, soft brown eyes. By this time next week, she'd be his wife. But what was she doing here now? "I was just getting ready to come pick you up."

She flipped long, sun-kissed brown hair from her shoulder and gave him one of her please-go-along-with-me smiles. "We have to break the date. Some things I have to do...about the house. It'll be late before I get through. Would you keep Jamie tonight? He...gets underfoot."

Averting a glance, she tried to hide a look of something that didn't belong in her eyes. Uncertainty? Fear? When her gaze returned to his, the look was gone.

"Sure, he can stay." Ben ruffled the seven-year-old's tawny hair. "We'll bach it tonight. There's a game on the TV. Go see if you can find it, buddy, and I'll hustle us up some grub."

Before Jamie darted off, Kelly grabbed him, hugging him tight enough to make the boy squirm.

She released Jamie and lifted her glance to Ben. That look was back in her doe-colored eyes and a film of tears. He took her hand and pulled her closer. "Is something wrong?"

Kelly laughed and pressed her other hand on top of his. She leaned in and nuzzled the side of his neck with a kiss, making him forget everything. Her arms found their way around his middle, and his mouth found hers.

She broke his hold. "Only God knows how much I love you."

"Me too...I mean, I love you, too." He ought to think of something better than that, but she had a way of muddling his thoughts.

"I have to go. There's a lot to do."

"Can I help?"

"All I ask is that you keep my son." She took the two steps to the door.

He came up behind and reached around her to open the door. "We'll pick you up for church in the morning."

"I'll be ready." She brushed his lips once more and ran down the steps.

Ben closed the door and made his way to the bathroom. "Hey, buddy, watch the TV until I get out of the shower, okay?"

"'Kay," Jamie said.

The water was cold now, but Ben had to make it short, so he lathered and was just pulling on his pants when the phone rang. Anyone but Kelly could wait.

Except Dave, his lawyer.

His swiped the phone with a still damp finger. "Yeah, Dave."

David Sims sounded on the other end. "Ready to get married, Ben?"

"More than ready."

"I finished my investigation into Jamie's adoption, and it's been approved." Ben had thought the adoption would have to take place after he and Kelly married. Silence hung between them for several seconds. "If you've changed your mind—"

"No. Dave, I just wasn't expecting it so soon. I'm ready, but it is a little jarring to learn I've just become a legal father. You are coming to the wedding, aren't you, Dave?"

"Sure, Ben. I'm here for you, man."

"Thanks."

"Are you still planning on moving to Atlanta?"

"Right after Kelly and I get back from our honeymoon to Cancun. Jan and Bill Garland, next door, will take care of Jamie, and when we get back, all three of us will be off."

Dave laughed. "Leave it to an accountant to measure everything down to the minute."

"It won't be at the minute, but we'll leave soon after. I have to report in May."

A swish sounded over the phone, followed by another of Dave's chuckles. "The warmest part of the year."

"So?"

"They don't call it Hotlanta for nothing."

"I expect we'll get acclimated in time. You come visit sometimes."

"I will. I travel through the Atlanta airport a lot."

"Call ahead, and we'll have you for dinner. We're getting a house in one of the suburbs. And, Dave, thank you for all you did to get the papers through on Jamie. Kelly will be thrilled."

"Kelly already knows. I hope I didn't let any cat out of the bag. She might have wanted to tell you."

Kelly knew? Why didn't she tell him at the door? "I won't let on, Dave, and thanks again."

Ben decided not to tell Jamie until Kelly was present. This was something the three of them should share. Maybe that's why she didn't tell Ben.

Well, a father was responsible for feeding his kid. He trekked to the kitchen and assembled what little he had for supper.

"Better eat up." Ben nudged the fruit cup closer to Jamie's plate.

The boy nibbled on a wiener. "We have hotdogs sometimes with buns and slaw."

Ben's mouth quirked a grin. Leave it to kids to be honest. "Sorry, I didn't have buns, and slaw is beyond me." He had fried some potatoes, the only other thing left in the pantry. Maybe he should have ordered pizza.

Jamie's small fingers worked to get the plastic lid off the fruit cup. "Mom said everything was fixed so you could 'dopt me after you get married."

Ben took the fruit cup. They ought to make the lids easier for a child to open. He took his time to pry the top off, stalling for time to choose his words carefully.

Jamie was an abused child. Kelly had married his father straight out of high school because she had to. Jamie was three months old when Craig Moon started shaking and striking the baby. When Kelly intervened, he turned his rage on her. When Jamie was six, Kelly mustered the nerve to leave Craig. They were divorced, but she couldn't get rid of him.

Incredibly, though he'd been arrested twice for child abuse, he was given visitation rights.

When Ben started dating Kelly, he knew if the

relationship grew, it would include Jamie. The boy drank up his attention like a parched flower. With a great deal of patience, he'd drawn Jamie out of his shell. He'd taken the boy camping, fishing, and taught him to play ball. Did all the guy things Kelly couldn't.

Ben finished ripping the plastic lid off, contemplating how to tell the boy without exactly telling him. "Your dad signed the papers giving up his parental rights, so your mom and I should have the adoption papers soon."

"And I won't have to go with him anymore?"

There was so much fear remaining in Jamie's voice, Ben scraped the chair back and moved around the table. He lifted the boy in his arms. "That's right. I'll be your dad from now on."

Jamie's arms tightened around Ben's neck and he felt tears on his cheek—his and Jamie's.

They overslept the next morning, and Ben chided himself, but it was a night of celebrations of sorts, though Jamie didn't know the adoption was final. Probably didn't matter. He was still at the age when a promise was as good as a deed.

But he shouldn't have let Jamie stay up playing computer games. Cereal would have to do for breakfast. The doorbell caught him before he reached the kitchen.

Kelly must have decided to join them here. Eagerness quickened his steps to the door.

A policeman stood on the stoop. That was enough to give anyone a jolt, and Ben held his breath, not able to speak.

The officer took off his hat. "Are you Ben Lucas?"

Ben nodded.

"Kelly Moon's neighbor said you're engaged to Mrs. Moon."

Ben finally found his voice. "That's right. Won't you come in?"

"No." The officer looked down at his hat. "I hate this job." He raised his gaze. "I regret to tell you your fiancée was killed last night."

Ben swallowed. The words hung in the air, not penetrating to his brain. "An accident?"

"No accident. Her ex murdered her."

"But you have him?"

"He's dead. It was a murder/suicide. I'm sorry, Mr. Lucas. We can't locate any other relatives."

"I...I'll take care of...everything."

Ben closed the door and stumbled to the bedroom. *Why did you let this happen, God?*

But God didn't do this—an evil man did.

His gaze swept the room that was to be theirs and landed on a black metal wastebasket. When he'd asked Kelly how she wanted to change the bedroom before she moved in, she said the wastebasket had to go. He focused all his rage on that basket.

After kicking it across the room, he stomped it again and again until it was a flattened mess of metal and paper. In less time than it had taken him to destroy the wastebasket, evil had snuffed out a beautiful and loving woman, taken his future, his heart—

The door slammed open, jerking him around. Jamie stared at him with frightened doe-like eyes—her eyes.

Ben's knees buckled and he fell to the floor. A power greater than himself stretched his arms out to the little boy.

Jamie slammed into him, and they clung to each other.

The next week passed in a fog. Ben might as well have been a robot, mechanically doing all the things that had to be done. Monday morning he stood at the window, staring at a vibrant spring day and seeing nothing. He should have been on his honeymoon.

"Time to get up, Jamie. You'll have to help me pack today."

Grief came by degrees for both of them. Denial. Anger. Acceptance. The numbness in the pit of Ben's soul must be acceptance, but he'd be working on that a long time.

Ben felt a tug on his pants and wasn't surprised to find Jamie beseeching him with those large, brown, soulful eyes. The child hadn't been more than a few steps away from him during the whole ordeal. He'd crawled into Ben's bed at night.

"What's going to happen to me? Wh...where am I going?" Jamie's lips trembled on the words.

Ben picked him up and took him to the sofa. He set Jamie on his lap. "You're not going anywhere, buddy. Remember, I showed you the adoption papers. I'll put them in a picture frame and hang it in our new house in Atlanta."

The muscles in Jamie's throat quivered as he gulped. "So you're going to keep me?"

She had known. *All I ask is that you keep my son.* She had known there'd be a confrontation and had brought Jamie to him to keep him safe—possibly to save Ben, too.

"Sure I'm keeping you. I'm your dad."

Ben had already worked out the anger—at Craig, at God, at himself for not protecting her. Nothing was left but hope that good would always triumph evil.

Somehow God had given him peace—and a son.

Chapter 1

Atlanta, Georgia, Six Months Later

Trust in the Lord with all your heart, and lean not on your own understanding. - Proverbs 3:5

My life was all planned out for the next three years. Then I met a man named Ben.
-Rebecca Atkins

Rebecca Atkins looked around the Sunday School classroom and then down to her clipboard. She liked matching faces to names—the best way to remember them. There was Ted Green, the teacher, a divorced man with three children who lived across the country. Janice Marshal, a divorcee with two children and trying to make ends meet on a waitress's wages and tips. Carla and Marsha Zimmerman, never married sisters, both hoping to be. Sammy Lyons, a mentally challenged man who lived with his mother. And Darcy Harkins, Rebecca's best friend, never married like her.

While Ted read the scripture that went with the lesson, Rebecca let her gaze linger on the newest member of the class, Ben Lucas. She didn't know anything about him except what he'd written on his enrollment card—and that his eyes were the softest and saddest gray she'd ever seen.

He was an accountant and had offered his services to needy members or carpentry jobs the church needed, though he wasn't skilled in that area.

Rebecca appreciated anyone willing to give of themselves. She could well relate to the scripture where the prophet said, "Here am I, send me." She'd done that herself when she'd moved to this church last year and asked if there was a singles department. Somehow, she'd volunteered to organize and direct it.

She'd never planned on being a leader, but that's the way it always happened. She'd been happy in her job as a chemist in one of the city's top chemical companies. Then she'd sent in her resume to Bay Pharmaceuticals for the position of director of Research. No one was more surprised than she when she got it, and now, after a six-month orientation program, she'd landed in the company's office building in the heart of the city.

It meant she had to move, but with her increased income she'd taken a spacious apartment in the high-rise near work.

But she also had to change churches and decided on Parkview Baptist, a smaller church in the nearby suburb of Haven. She'd divided the new Singles Sunday School into four classes. Young Adults, ages eighteen through twenty-five. It was the largest for obvious reasons. Twenty-six through forty was her group and made up of far too many divorced young people, only half of whom came regularly. Forty-one through sixty was a small group which included divorced and widowed. Finally, the sixty-plus, made up mostly of widows.

She bowed her head for the closing prayer, still wondering about Ben Lucas, and petitioned God to watch over him, though the reason wasn't exactly clear to her.

Ted ended the prayer and cleared his throat. "Before we leave, I think Rebecca has another project for us."

She got up and stepped into the middle of the circle. "One of our older church members had a stroke recently—Al Simmons—some of you may know him. He's able to come home, but his house has to be renovated to his new limitations—wheelchair ramp, widened doorways. Things like that. I need carpenters and workers who can take orders from carpenters."

A chuckle ran around the room. "Four out of the YA group have volunteered and two from the older group. Do I have any volunteers? Our workday will be Saturday, probably all day."

Darcy, Ted, and Marsha raised their hands and

Rebecca made a note. They always volunteered. She would be there, of course. She started to snap her log closed when Ben's soft baritone made her freeze. There was something about the man's voice that sent a mellow shaft through her.

"I might be able to if babysitting is available."

A giddy little shiver raced up Rebecca's spine. *Don't go there,* a voice warned. She'd resolved not to get involved with another man with baggage. His enrollment card told her he was single, not divorced or widowed, but with a seven-year-old son. It wasn't unheard of for a single woman to have a child, nor for a divorced man to have custody of a child, but a single man? For sure, he had baggage, and lots of it.

"The nursery will be open. Addie Hancock runs it for the church and the sweetest grandmother you'll ever meet." With some effort, Rebecca kept the excitement out of her voice while holding his gaze. "Do you have carpentry skills, Ben?"

"I'm not very skillful, but I did some renovations on my house."

Good. He owned his own house. He was financially stable. A lot of the men in the singles group were not. She gave herself a mental shake. Why was that important to her? "I'm going to say you do then, and your help will be much appreciated."

She sent her glance around the room. "We'll meet here at nine on Saturday. Those of you with children can get them settled into the nursery, then we'll go on to the site. Is that good?"

Everyone indicated it was, and Rebecca fell in step

with Darcy on their way to church services. "Do you know anything about Ben Lucas?" she asked after waiting for the others to get out of earshot.

Darcy grinned. "I know he's caught your attention."

"He has not—not any more than any other new member. I just wonder how he came to have a son if he's never been married."

"Oh, that's right, you weren't here when he introduced himself to the class. He was engaged to be married, only a week away from the wedding. This happened a few months ago, I think. Anyway, his fiancée was murdered."

Rebecca stopped in her tracks, making the couple behind her skirt around. No wonder there was such sadness in his eyes. "How?"

"He didn't say how, but he adopted her little boy. Isn't that so sweet? I almost cried." Darcy tipped her head back and put on that teasing look of hers. "He'll appeal to every single woman in church. If I hadn't already found my Sam, I'd be interested. Besides with all that money you're making in your new job I'm sure you could use a good accountant." She wagged her brows for emphasis.

Rebecca gave her a playful push back in the stream of pedestrians. "The problem is that new job of mine won't give me any time for man-chasing."

By now they were entering the sanctuary, so further discussion wasn't possible. Rebecca searched the congregation and found Ben several rows in front. She could tell by his broad shoulders and the way his brown hair curled around his collar. He wore his hair longer than most men, and an urge to run her fingers through those wavy locks hit her. Maybe Darcy was right. He had caught her attention.

Silly. He wasn't through grieving his loss. He wouldn't be looking for a love interest, not that she was either, she reminded herself.

Chapter 2

Do not fear, little flock, for it is your Father's good pleasure to give you the kingdom. -Luke 12:32

When you pray for God to move in your life, don't be surprised when He does.
-Ben Lucas

Ben apprised the new doorframe to Mr. Simmons bathroom. All he had left to do was stain the wood.

Ted came down the hall holding a bucket of walnut stain and brush. "Looks like I'm just in time. Why don't you let me finish up here? You haven't even taken a break since lunch. I know the girls still have the coffee on."

"Sounds good to me." Ben wiped his hands on his jeans and slapped Ted on the back as he headed toward the kitchen from where feminine chatter drifted.

As he turned the corner, he almost collided with Rebecca Atkins. She finger-combed a stray tendril off her cheek, smoothing her long dark brown hair, lit with red highlights. A smile tipped the corners of her full lips. "I was just coming to see if you'd finished. How about some coffee?"

Their glances met and he read something in her eyes he hadn't seen in a long time. Admiration? No, she was just a congenial woman. Don't read more into it than is there, and besides, his heart wasn't ready for that. "Thank you, I'd appreciate a cup and a brownie if one's left."

She turned, then gave him a backward look. "I saved one for you. Brownies are about the only thing I can bake fit to eat."

"I don't believe that."

She took a paper cup and poured the dark brew. "It's a little strong. Do you take cream or sugar?"

He was mesmerized by her dark blue eyes and sweeping lashes. She was a beautiful woman up close, even dressed in an old plaid shirt and jeans. "Uh, yes, just a little cream."

Darcy called from the back door. "I'm going to be leaving, guys."

Rebecca tore her gaze away. "Oh, thank you, Darce.

Call me after your date."

Darcy laughed. "You know I will."

Ben wondered if Rebecca dated anyone. Surely she did—a girl as pretty as she was. He'd find out soon enough. This close-knit group didn't keep any secrets. It occurred to him he could ask her out and find out for himself, but he rejected that. He wanted to hold onto Kelly's memories a little while longer.

But there was Jamie to think about. He needed a mother.

Ben munched on the brownie and sipped his coffee while Rebecca cleaned the coffee pot and packed up the remains of the foodstuffs.

Ted joined them. "Well, that's it. Looks pretty good, don't you think?"

Rebecca squeezed his arm. "You've all done a wonderful job, Ted. Mr. Simmons will be delighted."

Were Ted and Rebecca an item? That thought sent a little dart of something akin to jealousy through Ben. Not the usual jealousy. Ted was a nice guy, and he and Rebecca made a nice couple. No, Ben was jealous of every couple because they had what was taken from him.

"Couldn't have done it without this guy." Ted punched Ben on the arm. "He's a good carpenter."

Ben swallowed the last of his brownie. "Ted's no slouch, either."

"You're both a blessing to the church," Rebecca said as Ted departed.

Ben tossed his empty cup in the trash bag. "I'll carry this to the can on my way out."

Rebecca dove into her handbag and jingled keys. "I'll lock up right after you."

"See you next Sunday, then." Knowing he'd have to pick up Jamie, Ben hurried out, but seeing loose boards scattered along the yard, decided to gather them. He'd put them in his truck and discard them at his house. Mr. Simmons's trash can was overflowing.

He was about to climb in his truck when shrill screams rent the air. Jumping back, he ran in their direction.

Seated in the driver's seat of her navy sedan, Rebecca stared straight ahead, her features congealed in terror. Ben observed her through the open car door. She seemed to be frozen, hands clenching the steering wheel, and screaming like a girl watching a horror flick.

Ben darted a glance one way and then the other. He saw nothing that would have caused her fright. He swung the door wide open. Breathing rapidly, Rebecca's frozen gaze didn't budge. Was she having a seizure?

He grabbed her shoulder. "Rebecca, what is it?"

She gulped in fast and deeply, clearly hyperventilating. "There...there..."

He followed the line of her vision. On the windshield was what appeared to be a giant spider. Solid black, it wasn't like any garden spider Ben had ever seen. The only black spider he knew of was the black widow, but this one was way too big.

Women were known to be skittish around spiders,

and he agreed this was a big one, but it was outside the windshield. Rebecca's hysteria was beyond reasonable. She was shaking uncontrollably and would pass out if she kept hyperventilating.

He released her and tapped on the windshield, then realized the spider wasn't even real. He ducked out of the car, reached around, and plucked the toy off the glass. Taking a step back, he examined the thing. Just a plastic toy such as kids played with at Halloween. Meant to scare people, but Rebecca's reaction was over the top. She would laugh when she saw the truth.

She didn't laugh when he thrust it at her. In fact, her screams pierced his eardrums. "It's just plastic, Rebecca!" he shouted, but his words obviously weren't getting through.

He jerked around and started to fling the toy away, but decided she wouldn't calm down until he got rid of it. Since he obviously couldn't "kill" it for her, he held it high over his head and jogged to the garbage can, stuffing it inside. He hoped she could see it had been dispatched, or at least hear when he slammed the lid down.

When he returned, her head was resting on the steering wheel, and her shaking actually vibrated the car. He scratched his head, wondering what to do. He couldn't leave her like this. Despite her fear being imagined, her reaction was very real and serious.

After prying her fingers from the steering wheel, he tugged her out of the car. Holding her by the shoulders, he gave her a little shake. "It's all right, Rebecca. Can you hear me? You're safe now."

Rebecca held on to him. "Can't breathe...can't..."

He looked over her shoulder into the car and saw the plastic bags holding the kitchen supplies. Twisting around, he reached in and emptied one of them. He wedged her against the car, bunched the bag's opening in one hand and placed it over her mouth. "Breathe in the bag, slowly."

She fought him a few seconds before going limp. He caught her, cradling her in his arms. Her head lolled back, long, dark lashes cutting crescents on her pale cheeks as her chest rose and fell in a more normal rhythm. Maybe it was a good thing she'd passed out.

Water. He needed water to bring her around.

Holding her close, Ben looked around for the outside water spigot he'd seen earlier. He spotted it on the side of the house and strode that way. It occurred to him he hadn't held a woman this close since Kelly, and this was the first time the thought of Kelly didn't stab him with the sharp edge of grief.

He dropped to his knees at the spigot, wishing he had something to hold the water. Carefully laying her down, he slipped his left hand under her head, and turned the faucet with his right.

The water gushed, and he caught a palmful, pouring it over Rebecca's white face. Almost immediately, her eyes flew open. Her breathing had already returned to normal, but she looked dazed.

"Is everything all right?" He put a smile in his voice. "Are you sick?"

Her gaze darted around as if disoriented, then lit

on his face. "I think I can get up now," she said, her voice barely above a whisper.

Ben helped her to her feet, supporting her until he was sure she could stand. "If you'll give me the key, I can go back inside and get you a cup of water."

She shook her head, an action that had her flaying her arms to grab him. When she steadied, a nervous laugh slipped out, and she sent him an embarrassed look. "I'm all right now. Thank you. I can't believe how I overreacted to a plastic spider." Her smile held while she spoke. "I'd appreciate it if you didn't tell anyone. It's rather embarrassing." She walked out of his hold and started toward her car.

He could understand her embarrassment, but no way could he let her drive in her condition. It took three strides to catch up with her. "I don't think you're well enough to get in traffic yet." He glanced at his watch and grimaced. "Look, I have to pick up Jamie. The nursery was supposed to close at six." It was ten after. "How about we get him and go to the barbecue place at the end of the street? It might ruin your plans for dinner, but after a leisurely meal, you'll be back to normal."

Her glance bore into him like she couldn't decide if he could be trusted. "I've bothered you enough. I wouldn't want to ruin your plans for the evening."

Surely she didn't think he was trying to pick her up. "My plans were to get a pizza and go home. I'm in the mood for barbecue. What do you say?"

"Well...if you're sure I'm not interfering with any plans. I don't want you to think I was putting on an act to get your attention." She laughed. "Fainting like the heroine of some Victorian play."

Like a relief valve, her laughter released the tension between them. "I didn't think anything of the sort. You couldn't have been putting on an act if you were the best actor on Broadway." He smiled and laid a hand over her shoulder. "And you're not interfering at all. Jamie and I will enjoy the company." They walked to his jeep, and he helped her into the passenger side.

Chapter 3

The end of a thing is better than its beginning; the patient in spirit is better than the proud in spirit. -Ecclesiastes 6:4

I feel like the child who must look at the cake throughout a meal of vegetables and liver. - Rebecca Atkins

Rebecca watched Ben enter the church's annex through the truck's window. She felt more like a fool than that time she'd thought Darcy knocked on her bedroom door and opened it wearing nothing but her underwear and finding Jason standing there. No, this was worse. That was just a mistake. This revealed her...condition, something bordering on crazy, or at least that's what Ben must think.

Despite that, another emotion was taking over. Excitement. He'd asked her to dinner. As bizarre as the circumstance was, it threw them together, and she couldn't remember when she'd wanted to be thrown together with a man more.

In a matter of minutes, Ben came out the same door, holding the hand of a small tow-haired boy who skipped along. They came around to her side, and the boy halted, tilting his head up, he stared straight at her with big, brown eyes. He pointed a finger. "Who's that?"

Ben opened the back door. "This is Ms. Atkins, a nice lady who's going to have dinner at the *Rib Shack* with us. Up you go, buddy. Let's get the seatbelt on." Ben got in and sent her a glance. "That's my son, Jamie, Rebecca."

She twisted around in her seat. "Pleased to meet you, Jamie. Did you have fun today?"

"Yes, ma'am." His voice turned into a whine. "But you were late, Dad. I was the only one left."

"That was my fault, Jamie," Rebecca said. "I had a little trouble with a spider."

"I don't like spiders," Jamie said. "I like frogs. I have one named Ernie." He paused a moment, twisting his lips. "I have a turtle, too. I've had him for a long time, so long I don't remember when we got him. Guess what my mom named him?"

"Oh, I can't guess. I'm not good at guessing. You tell

me."

"Speedy." Jamie's childish laughter spilled forth. "Isn't that funny?"

Ben had maneuvered into the traffic easily, but Rebecca noticed out of the corner of her eye when he clenched his jaw. She decided to turn the conversation away from mention of Jamie's mother. "It is a funny, but a perfect one. I like turtles, especially giant sea turtles. I once saw hatchlings running into the sea right after they were born."

"Really? We go to the beach every year, but I've never seen a sea turtle."

"Well, maybe you will one day." Rebecca turned back around. Jamie was an adorable child, but he didn't look anything like his father, though Ben was adorable, too, in a manly sort of way.

It wasn't far to the restaurant, and they entered the busy eatery with its seat-yourself tables. They found the last empty booth. Rebecca sat on one side and Ben and Jamie on the other.

After the waitress brought water and took their order, Jamie tugged Ben's shirtsleeve. "Dad, can I play some games." They were seated near the place where several mechanical games were situated.

"Now Jamie, we've talked about that before. If you use your allowance money you may. Otherwise, no."

Jamie's countenance fell. "I left my allowance at home."

Ben sighed, then retrieved four quarters from his pocket. "You can have these if you pay me back when we get home."

"I don't have any quarters, just two dollar bills, and you said I have to save one."

Rebecca sipped her water and smiled at Ben's dilemma.

"You remember our math lesson?" Ben held out his hand with the quarters in his palm. "Your dollar is worth how many of these quarters?"

Jamie made a show of counting the quarters, his brows scrunched. Rebecca could almost see the wheels spinning in his mind. "Four. My dollar is worth all four."

Ben chuckled and pressed the quarters in his son's hand. "That's right. You come back when they're gone and don't expect any more." Jamie closed his small fingers over the coins and scampered from his seat. "And don't forget to pay me back later." Ben sent this parting shot after Jamie.

Rebecca laughed. "Anyone can tell you're a wonderful father, and Jamie is so cute. He must look like his mother." She clamped her lips shut. Why did she remind him of that?

Ben propped his elbows on the table. "Too cute to look like me?"

She relaxed. He had a sense of humor. "No, of course I didn't mean that. It's just he's blond and you're dark and—" She wasn't through stuffing her foot in her mouth.

"I'm not Jamie's natural father, Rebecca."

Her mouth fell open. "Oh, I'm sorry. I didn't mean anything." She felt heat rising in her neck and gulped from her water glass. Of course she meant it. How could he have custody of a son unless he had some...was the boy's father.

"I adopted him about the time Kelly— When she died."

Admiration mixed with mortification rushed through her. Dummy. That's what Darcy had told her. That spider incident had addled her brain. "I...that's wonderful—a wonderful thing to do."

"It wasn't easy. I was blessed. Though single parents are allowed to adopt, it's still not easy. But Jamie didn't have any blood relatives left—none who wanted him."

She reached across the table to grasp his arm. "And he's so blessed to have you. No one would realize you weren't his natural father."

"Except I don't look like him. But I'm the one's who's blessed, and I love him like I would my own flesh and blood."

She realized she was still touching him and pulled her hand back. "Please forgive me for being so brash."

He smiled. "It's all right, really. You won't mind if I'm a little personal with you, I hope. Why are you afraid of spiders?"

She just stared at him for a moment. It was something she guarded from most people, but something about this man made her want to trust him. "My father locked me in an old shed he said was full of spiders to punish me once. There were webs everywhere but no spiders actually got on me. It didn't matter. I was terrified because when I younger I almost died of a spider bite. I was about the same age as Jamie when I was shut in the shed."

She laughed lightly. "Before that time I was bitten, I'd played with all kinds of bugs. I was something of a tomboy."

The waitress brought them iced tea, and Ben drank long before asking, "How did that happen—that you were bitten?"

"It was a black widow. I'm sure of that because I was fascinated by the red dot. Actually, I played with it for a while before flicking it away. Trouble was, I didn't notice where it landed and rolled over and it bit me on the back of my thigh. It didn't hurt much at first, just like a mosquito bite. When I ran into the house, things turned black, and the place started throbbing. The last thing I remembered was my mother giving me mouth-to-mouth resuscitation and praying."

The compassion in his eyes urged her to continue, revealing more than she'd intended. "I know I was miraculously healed, Ben. I was very young and probably got things mixed up in my mind, but it was a black widow that bit me, and I did pass out. When I regained consciousness, my leg was swollen twice its size and was burning intensely, but by bedtime that night, it had gone back to normal, and the pain ebbed away."

She was probably making a mess of this witness. Strange, she'd never told anyone that part either. How she was healed. "I know spider bites aren't usually fatal, even in young children, but I still believe I'd have died if the Lord hadn't healed me."

"I believe you. Sounds like a miracle to me. It's understandable you'd be afraid of spiders. A lot of people suffer from arachnophobia."

A lot of women, he meant. Tears rose in her eyes and she pressed a paper napkin to the corners. "What I don't understand is how I could be physically healed like that, but assaulted with this fear. God doesn't send a spirit of fear, so it must be from Satan, but why did God allow that? And why can't I rid myself of it? Normally it's easy to avoid spiders, so I just ignore it."

Ben surprised her by reaching across the table to take her hand. "One thing you can be sure of, Rebecca, God allows things to happen for a purpose, even if we can't see it."

"You believe that?"

He patted her hand and laid it down. "I have to. It's the only thing that keeps me sane."

"How did your fiancée die, if you don't mind talking about it?"

"She was being stalked by her ex-husband." He looked down at the tiled floor like he did mind talking about it. With an audible sigh, his gaze found hers again.

"He even shot through her window while I was there the day before she was killed. After reporting the incident to the police, she wanted me to leave. Didn't want me involved, she said. She wanted to finish some things with the house. We set up a dinner date, but she came by later and broke it, leaving Jamie with me for the night. I should have known something was wrong. I blame myself."

He fell silent until she asked, "Why?"

That sadness she'd first noticed filled his eyes. "The thing is, I knew deep inside he would come back. She knew it, too. That's why she wanted me to take Jamie. I can't get rid of the guilt for not staying and somehow protecting her. Maybe I can deal with it someday. In the meantime, all I can do is be the best father I can be to Jamie and keep praying."

"I'm so sorry, Ben. My problem seems so shallow compared to yours."

"No, it's not shallow. I can tell you're a strong woman. You'll conquer this thing some day after it's served its purpose."

She searched his face. Was that the answer? God was letting her struggle with this fear to strengthen her for a purpose. Maybe because all other fears seemed so trivial in comparison. Fear of public speaking? She'd conquered that. Fear of leading? She'd overcome that, too. God worked in mysterious ways. He'd healed her mysteriously, but many times He withheld healing. Could it be for a larger purpose? She wanted to discuss this further with Ben, but Jamie came running back to the table at that moment.

"Look Dad, I won this." He thrust out a small plastic globe and popped it open. A toy bug fell on the table.

Rebecca flinched before Jamie scooped it up. "It's not a spider. It's a beetle. Know why? It has six legs and spiders have eight. I learned that on the *Science Channel*."

Ben exchanged a knowing smile with her that said, "Watch out for big ears." Jamie had apparently overheard her talk of spiders.

"You're a very smart boy. I know it's a beetle. I'm a scientist myself—not a biologist—a chemist."

Jamie's eyes widened. "Really? Like on the *Science Channel*?"

Here was a way to win the boy over, and she'd take it, although she didn't know why she wanted to win the boy over. "Yes, just like them, except I don't talk on TV. I do guest lecture at schools around the country, though, and present experiments." She lifted her glance to Ben. "If your dad doesn't mind, maybe you could come visit my department, and I'll introduce you to my science team. They can show you around their labs."

Their meal arrived at that moment, saving Ben from having to make an immediate commitment. All three got down to doing serious damage to pulled pork sandwiches and fries.

As Rebecca's physical hunger lessened, her hunger to become a part of Ben and Jamie's life grew. He hadn't asked for her phone number yet. Would he? Should she take the initiative? No guts, no glory was one of her favorite sayings. She opened her handbag and took out a card. In a bold move she'd never taken with any other man, she slid it across the table to Ben. "This is my business card. If you ever need a babysitter, give me a call. It's the least I can do to pay you back for helping me tonight."

It was a lame excuse, but she really would enjoy taking care of Jamie. Ben took the card. "You work in the Lowell Building?"

"Yes, I'm the Research Branch manager for Bay Pharmaceuticals." How snooty that sounded. She hastened to add, "Brand new, in fact. I took the position just last month."

"Is that right? The eleventh floor, right? I'm with Jenkins Accounting on the third floor. Surprised I've never met you. I thought I'd seen you around. A pretty girl like you is hard to forget."

She swallowed the laugh in her throat, knowing it would come out like a giggle. If there was one thing a branch manager or a prospective girlfriend couldn't do, it was giggle. "You're kidding? I knew Jenkins was in the same building, but I've never seen you." Not that she would with the hours she kept—seven-to-seven.

"I rarely ever go above the third floor."

"And I've only been there a month. It's a big building."

"It is. There must be six hundred employees on my floor alone."

"I don't know how many are on my floor, maybe the same."

"I doubt it. The eleventh floor is the one with office suites. We have mainly cubicles, though I recently got my own small office." He drained his tea glass and the attentive waitress was at his hand refilling it. When the attendant left, he added, "I'm a small business accountant."

"I'll keep that in mind. I don't have a business, but I should get an accountant before tax season."

Ben took the time to wipe catsup off Jamie's face. He brought out his wallet and slipped a card from its contents and held it wedged between two fingers. Rebecca accepted his business card with a smile. "I can do personal taxes, too."

She scrutinized the card for a moment. "I can't believe we work in the same building."

"And you're a manager on eleventh heaven?"

"'We bring in the best minds to work on cures for the worst diseases.' That's our motto. Actually, the entire floor is research—chemical and biological."

"A noble job." There was a note of teasing in Ben's voice. "I just keep people out of tax court."

"Well, that goes to the quality of life as much as healing does."

"Dad, can we go soon?" Jamie asked, his eyes getting heavy.

Ben checked his watch. "It's later than I realized. Good we can sleep a little late tomorrow, but we still have church."

Rebecca stood. The time had passed much too fast for her. She frowned.

"Do you feel better now?" Ben asked. "Your coloring is certainly better."

"Yes, I'm fine, and the traffic has thinned out by now. Thank you for inviting me to join you two. I've enjoyed it."

"We've enjoyed it too, haven't we, buddy?"

"Is Ms. Atkins going home with us?"

Rebecca laughed. "No, you're going to drop me off at my car and I'll be on my way, but maybe we can do this again some time." Did she really say that? There was just something about this man and his son that made her want to spend more time with them.

She had reached the I-285 connector before reality set in. For the next several months she couldn't think about dating. She had enemies at Bay Pharmaceuticals, men who had been expecting to land that management job. Men who didn't think a young woman was qualified. She'd have to spend every free moment learning her new job.

Proving herself.

Chapter 4

**For you are still carnal. For where there
are envy, strife, and division among you,
arc you not carnal and behaving like mere
men. –1 Corinthians 3:3**

*I always expect either too much of a man or too
little. In the end, both good and bad are just men,
and I cannot judge them any more than they can
judge me—just a woman. –Rebecca Atkins*

If there were a time for falling in love in Georgia it
would be October. Late summer and early fall blended
into a perfect setting—deep blue, cloudless skies, crisp

mornings, followed by golden daylight and dreamy moonlit nights.

God's timing was perfect, Rebecca reminded herself, even when hers wasn't. If He wanted her to get together with Ben Atkins, He'd work it out. Until then, she'd forget about it, no matter how yummy Ben was and how perfect the setting.

That's what her brain told her, but her heart was having none of it. For that reason, she'd try to carve out a bit of time every weekend and maybe a loose hour here and there during the week.

With that objective at the back of her mind, she'd stayed up until two o'clock last night studying employee files, the twenty-six scientists, anyway. The office staff wasn't a great concern. But she'd get to know all of them, study their likes, dislikes, get to know their families, pray for them. Before she was through, she'd know her subordinates better than their mamas did.

Too bad she'd forgotten to set her alarm. She was seriously late.

Ignoring her stomach's grumbling for her usual egg and jelly biscuit and coffee, she rushed right past her favorite café, making good time in the heavy pedestrian traffic. The Lowell building was only a ten-minute walk from her apartment building. Thank goodness, she didn't have to drive like all those people sitting in grid-lock behind the wheel of their automobiles.

When the elevator reached the eleventh floor, Rebecca remembered how Ben referred to it as eleventh heaven. If he only knew how tense things could get up here. She stepped out and her heels clicked rapidly on the highly polished floor leading to her office.

Margaret Thames, her personal secretary, was on the phone as Rebecca nodded to her. The large mahogany door swung easily on its hinges, opening to her inner office. In a way, it was heaven. Tall windows revealed the city skyline and sunlight spilled over the plush carpet. Rebecca hung up her coat and crossed the room to her desk.

A package sat in the middle of her glossy blotter. Strange, only one reason Margaret wouldn't have opened it. It must be personal. It certainly wasn't unusual for Rebecca to get personal mail—but a package?

The thing was about twelve inches square and all sorts of postal markings covered the surface. Her curiosity turned to trepidation as she read the marks. Inspected by Customs Officer 1072. Caution. Live Animals. She could tell the entire top was perforated with tiny holes.

Clearly this was a mistake. The package should have been delivered to the labs in Biological Research. The smaller print on the top seemed to jump out at her. Taragenda Spiders.

She jerked back, almost tripping over her chair. Don't be silly. Even if it contained spiders, and even if they were the most poisonous in the world, they couldn't get out.

Unless they already were.

Impossible. The package was definitely sealed on all sides—except a narrow wire mesh breathing strip.

But there was the bottom.

Rebecca jumped when the door swooshed. Margaret came in with a steaming cup of coffee. "Isn't this a beautiful morning." She set the cup on the trivet on Rebecca's desk. Her eyes narrowed as they focused on the package. "What's this?" Margaret asked.

"It says it's spiders from South America. Did you see who delivered it?"

"No—I haven't seen any delivery men or anyone this morning. The door was locked as usual when I arrived. You weren't expecting it, I take it?"

"Absolutely not. Will you take it? No, wait—I'll call Davidson. It obviously belongs in his department. He ought to know about the mix-up. Delivery men are expected to get a signature for deliveries like this—or they should. Anyway, if it's an infraction. Davidson must know."

Margaret smiled and started for the door. "Oh, Margaret, one other thing. When I was going over the personnel files last night, I didn't notice anything on my predecessor, Mr. Moran. Do you know why?"

"I believe the personnel department swept the files before you arrived."

"Swept the files?"

"Yes, Mr. Moran time was expunged from the records." She laughed like that was a common occurrence. "He was just sitting in temporarily anyway as I understand it. You have been the official Chief of Chem from the moment of your assignment, all through your tour of orientation."

That was news to Rebecca. She only hoped she wouldn't wind up expunged. "Thank you, Margaret."

"I'll get Mr. Davidson on the phone for you," Margaret said as she backed out the door.

Harold Davidson was head of Neuropharmacology Research in Bio. Rebecca hadn't had many dealings with him, but those few times, he had been affable and professional. He came across as intelligent—certainly not someone she'd expect to run a sloppy outfit.

"Tell him to come on in—as soon as possible." With one finger, Rebecca pushed the package to the edge of the desk and sank into her plush chair. She opened a folder and tried to concentrate, but found herself rereading the same page of the report twice.

The buzzer sounded. "Yes, Margaret."

"Mr. Davidson is here."

"Send him in, please."

Davidson, a tall, darkly handsome African-American entered. "I hope I'm not in any trouble." He laughed and took the side chair.

"Not at all." Rebecca gestured to the package. "I found this box of spiders on my desk this morning. Obviously it belongs in Bio. Do you have any idea why it was sent to me?"

Davidson took the box and inspected it. "None at all. It's clearly addressed to my department. The delivery man must have made a mistake."

"It would seem so. Don't you require such deliveries to be signed for?"

"We do." He frowned. "The ticket has been torn off, so I assume someone did sign for it." He gave her a level stare. "I'll get to the bottom of this."

"I've no doubt you will. Is everyone in the department authorized to sign for deliveries?"

"Yes, but maybe I should change that to division heads."

"I think that would be advisable, not for every delivery, but certainly for specimens."

"I'll change the policy, effective today. Is there anything else, Ms. Atkins?" He got to his feet.

Rebecca stood and reached out to shake his hand. "Just take this with you, and thank you for coming so promptly."

Davidson started across the room, then pivoted. "Oh, I forgot to tell you. I hired a new scientist, Derek Gammon. Heard of him?"

The name did sound familiar, but Rebecca couldn't place him at the moment. "It's possible. I might even have met him. Gammon rings a bell."

"His credentials are impeccable. He was in contention for the position you hold. Maybe that's why he sounds familiar to you."

"That's likely. We might have met at the interview panel, but there was a roomful of applicants. I still can't believe I was selected."

"Don't sell yourself short, Ms. Atkins. You have a great resume and Dr. Breckenridge said your interview score was the third highest in the country."

She knew. That's what had put her in contention, but words like that always made her feel humble. How had she acquired this job when so many others were seemingly better qualified? Dr. Breckenridge had assured her it was because she had something one couldn't attain through education or experience—perception.

Davidson had no sooner left when her private line chimed. A dart of hope speared her. Maybe it was Ben. "Hello."

"Hey, Rebecca, I've moved back to Atlanta. So, how're you doing?"

Jason. He was back in town. Why would he think she'd ever want to hear from him again? "I've been doing fine. You?"

"Great. I heard you'd gotten a big promotion and are calling the shots at Bay Pharm. I'd like to hear all about it. Could we go out to dinner sometime this week?"

IIe had to be kidding. When Rebecca had broken up with Jason, she'd made it clear they had no future. Yes, at one time she'd expected they'd get married. That was before she knew all he wanted from her was a physical relationship—that didn't include marriage. She still chided herself for her stupidity. Apparently her perception had a blind spot.

"No, I don't think that would be a good idea. It's best we let things stay as they were."

"Ah, come on. You don't still blame me for making a pass?"

A pass? Was that what he called it? She recognized attempted rape when she saw it. She still thanked God for giving her an escape.

She wasn't quick enough to respond, and he went on, "You can find it in your heart to forgive me, can't you? You were a fine Christian."

He hit a nerve, and she felt her ire rising. So like Jason to jab at her Christianity. "I do forgive you, Jason, but we can't be friends. Now if you'll excuse me, I have a lot to do."

"Wait...don't hang up. At least let me try to make it up to you."

"There's nothing to make up. Good-bye, Jason. I wish you all the best." And she hoped he would find a woman who used him as he'd used Rebecca. She pressed the button to end the connection. Maybe that wasn't very Christian. She could forgive Jason, but wasn't yet at the point where she'd forget.

She turned her attention back to her computer, and the phone chimed again. After it went through its process four times, she pressed the receiver. "Listen Jason, I have nothing more to say."

"It's Ben, Rebecca."

Her anger switched to excitement in a flash. "I'm sorry, Ben. I was trying to get rid of someone."

His husky chuckle sent a shiver through her. "You obviously succeeded. I'm calling to see if you're feeling better."

Feeling better? She couldn't feel better. Oh, he meant had she recovered from her spider scare. "Yes,

Ben, I've recovered from my hysterics."

"Glad to hear it."

"Oh, and you won't believe what happened this morning. Someone had left a package from South America on my desk. Know what it contained?" She laughed. "Spiders—probably from the rain forest. They're purported to be the most poisonous in the world. I don't know if that's true or not, but what a coincidence."

She expected to hear his deep laugh. Instead, nothing but silence as the seconds ticked off. "Ben?"

"Yeah. Rebecca." Another long pause. "I go out for a walk every afternoon, just to get away from the office, get some fresh air. Would you join me this afternoon? Just tell me when you're free. I expect my schedule is a lot more flexible than yours."

A walk—with him? She clicked onto her schedule. Flexible or not, she'd find the time. "I'd like that. How about two forty-five. I have a meeting at three, but if I'm a little late..." She laughed again. "They can't start without me."

His soft, deep chuckle warmed her insides. "Two forty-five it is. I'll meet you in the lobby."

She ended the call and sank back into the chair's cushions. Suddenly the day looked a whole lot better.

Chapter 5

Be sober, be vigilant; because your adversary the devil walks about like a roaring lion, seeking whom he may devour. -1 Peter 5:8

If Satan wore a nametag, no one would be deceived. -Ben Lucas

Ben paced the length of the foyer, back and forth, glancing each turn at the elevator. Rebecca was only a few minutes late, but it didn't matter how late she was. He meant to talk to her. The more he thought about a package of spiders being left on her desk, the more uneasy he became.

That feeling of impending dread followed him like a shadow—the same way he'd felt the night of Kelly's murder. He had known deep in his gut Kelly was in danger. For the hundredth time he asked himself why he'd let her go that day. Maybe he couldn't have done anything. He might have been killed too. Jamie might have been killed.

Kelly had thought so. Try as he might, Ben couldn't shake the guilt that he'd abandoned her. Now that same urgency churned in his stomach. Why? He didn't really know Rebecca. She didn't have a crazy ex-husband stalking her. But someone might be stalking her.

She thought the package of spiders was a coincidence. He didn't believe in coincidence. Everything had a purpose. Was this God's way of giving him another chance—to protect a woman. Another chance at love?

There was chemistry between him and Rebecca. He'd felt it that first morning in the Sunday School class. The looks she gave him assured him she felt the chemistry, too. Strange that he'd notice it so quickly—almost at first sight. He'd been dating Kelly several weeks before he'd noticed the first tinges of attraction.

He wasn't ready to get involved in another relationship. Common sense told him to take it slow, but this business with the spiders called for immediate action. He just hoped Rebecca would take it seriously.

The ding of the elevator doors drew his attention again. Several people stepped out before he saw her. She turned her head, looking. They made eye contact and he felt a little jolt. There was definitely chemistry. She came toward him, smiling.

Rebecca wore a ruby wool dress reaching a couple of inches above the knee and hugging a curvaceous feminine shape. Her gray cloak swayed as she walked, and her high heels clicked on the marbled tile floor. Sensible shoes, not stilettos like some women tortured themselves with.

"Hi, sorry to keep you waiting."

"I haven't been waiting long." He just touched her back and followed her out the automatic door.

He pointed toward the right. "I usually walk to the atrium and fountain." The street wasn't crowded and they strode side-by-side.

Rebecca chatted easily about her day, and they were half way to the stopping place. He had to get to the point. "So, the package of spiders didn't faze you?"

She laughed. "No, I knew they were completely encased. Of course they were no doubt real—unlike that one last Saturday. No, no panic attacks today."

"It got me thinking. Does anyone hold a grudge against you? Maybe someone who knows you have a phobia of spiders."

She pulled back a step. "A grudge? You don't honestly believe someone might have deliberately put that package on my desk? And the plastic one?"

"I don't mean to sound paranoid, but yes, I have a bad feeling about this. Maybe it's nothing, but to ease my mind, would you tell me if someone could be stalking you?"

Her steps slowed, the smile wiped off her face. She shook her head and waves of dark brown, honey highlighted hair fell against her cheeks. Ben resisted the urge to brush it back. "Some old boyfriend?"

She shook the hair out of her face, setting it shimmering in the afternoon sunshine. "None who would do anything like that." A light came on in her eyes. "Except..." They both stopped. "Jason called just before you did to tell me he was back in town." She laughed—that same nervous laughter he'd noticed after her fright Saturday night.

"He wanted to get back together, but that's not happening."

"How well did you know Jason?"

"I thought he was the perfect...date...at one time. That's all he was, someone to escort me to functions. I admit I sometimes entertained the thought that it might lead to something more." She lifted her hands in a helpless gesture. "Trouble was, that something more meant marriage to me, to him it meant an affair. Before he went off to Europe, I made it clear I wanted nothing more to do with him."

"Apparently, he didn't accept that." Ben didn't like the sound of Jason, and he knew those types of men better than Rebecca did. If they thought they could score with a woman, they didn't easily give up the chase.

Despite Rebecca's education, professional position, and sophisticated style, he suspected she was pretty innocent.

"It doesn't make sense that he'd want to scare me with spiders."

"Did he know about your phobia?"

"Yes, of course, but if he wanted us to get back together, why would he want to scare me? Besides, he wouldn't have had access to the lab's spiders."

"Anyone who would have access? Someone who might want revenge?"

Her shapely lips twisted into a grimace. "There was Lyle Moran. I filled the position he was demoted from for making slurs against a visiting professor. He works in Bio now." She lifted her shoulders. "But I had nothing to do with his firing, and it's silly to think he'd follow me to a church function."

"Not if he were a stalker."

"Now you're scaring me."

Ben reached out and took her hand. It was ice cold so he covered it with the other. "I don't mean to scare you, but the feeling I have that something isn't right is strong. Maybe it's nothing. Just be alert. Aware of what's happening. If it is a stalker, he'll try again."

"But what can I do about it?"

He gave that some thought. What could she do? "You live in a secure building, so you should be safe there. Do you have a gun?"

"A gun? Good heavens, no."

"If anything else happens, it would be a good idea to get one and a permit to conceal. I'm not sure that's allowed in the city, but if you can get a permit, keep it in your handbag. I can get you some mace."

A clock chimed three o'clock. "I have to get back to

work," she said.

Rebecca took off like a shot, pivoting and rushing back toward their building. Ben had to jog briskly to keep up.

He'd upset her, and maybe she was trying to get away from him as much as getting back to work. He might have ruined his chances with her, but was still glad to have warned her.

Not a word was spoken as they rode the elevator. When he made to get off on the third floor, she touched his arm. "Thank you for your concern, Ben. I'm going to ask about Moran."

"Just be careful," was all he could get out as the door closed.

Chapter 6

Ointment and perfume delight the heart, and the sweetness of a man's friend gives delight by hearty counsel. -Proverbs 27:9

A true friend is one whom you can invite over without hiding the clutter in your house or your soul. -Rebecca Lucas

"So how are things going with you and that hot new accountant?" Darcy stood at the counter, whipping the potatoes. She and Rebecca cooked and ate dinner together most nights. They both liked to cook—Darcy did anyway—but it seemed senseless to cook for one person. Plus, the leftovers would pack their lunches for the next day.

Rebecca swiped her with a dishcloth. "Hot new accountant? I'll have to tell him that one." She returned to wiping down the island. "I assume you mean Ben."

"Don't play dumb with me, girl. I saw the way you looked at him in Sunday School class. He about gave you a cardiac."

Everyone who worked in the serious world of science should have a friend like Darcy. Someone to tease and cajole. Rebecca counted Darcy a great blessing, someone to bring her back to earth at the end of the day. And not afraid to tell her the truth.

She couldn't help a giggle as she met Darcy's stare. "He didn't give me a cardiac. I behaved quite naturally when we took a walk together today. He works in my building, you know."

"You mentioned that. So did you just run into each other?"

"He invited me. Actually, I think he was concerned about the spiders being left on my desk."

"Hand me the salt. It was crazy...I mean after you got scared of that toy spider at Mr. Simmons's."

Rebecca had told Darcy all about that. Now she wished she hadn't. "It was a coincidence, nothing more." She opened the oven door to peek at the roast. "I think the beef's done." She took the braised brisket, simmering in its own juices, out and set the pan on an iron crab-shaped trivet Mom had brought her from a trip to the Florida Keys.

"The green beans are done, too. I'll get the plates." Darcy had to stretch to reach the dinnerware. "I think it's sweet that Ben was concerned. You are going to encourage him, aren't you? I mean you aren't going to bury yourself in research and test tubes during this fine stretch of weather."

Rebecca waited until she'd popped four rolls under the broiler before answering. "I don't think I will encourage him. My job is much too demanding to get into a serious relationship, and I have a feeling Ben's the type who'd expect something serious, if anything at all."

Darcy looked up from across the island. "What's wrong with him? He's very good looking, and I thought you liked him."

"I do like him...it's just that, well, I'd prefer a casual relationship. Besides, I don't think I'm Ben's type."

"Why not. Sounds like he thinks you're his type." She snickered. "And he should know."

Rebecca took out the rolls and poured iced tea. "Just little things. He's like a lot of men who take their faith seriously." Darcy pointed a finger with another argument, but Rebecca warded her off with a raised hand. "Let's be honest, Darcy. We know sincere Christian men believe women should take a subordinate role in everything. Even if they work, they're supposed to depend on the man."

"You just met Ben. How can you know if that's what he believes?"

"Little jabs he made about me working on eleventh heaven. My position is higher than his. I probably make more than he does. You know, some men don't like that. In a way, his jumping in to protect me from what he perceives to be a danger proves he divides the roles of men and women sharply."

They both sat and Rebecca gave the grace. "In a way, I, too, believe married women should devote themselves to their home and family. That's why I don't see marriage in my immediate future." She served the beef to Darcy, then herself. "It's a serious consideration. Ben has a child."

"You said he's an adorable little boy."

"He is, and he needs a mother—a full time mother."

"Seems to me any mother would be better than none at all."

Rebecca shook her head. "I can't see myself as a mother. I know how hard it is. There are several young mothers working for me. They juggle childcare, nursing the baby, taking children to the doctor, attending school functions—and they're constantly worried about what's going on. Checking baby monitors, calling the sitter. Frankly, they can't devote their full attention to their jobs. I've committed myself to this position and until I get a foothold, it's going to take every ounce of my attention."

"Are you arguing with me or with yourself?"

Rebecca laughed and speared a piece of meat. "With myself, I suppose."

They ate in silence for a few minutes. "I wonder why Ben thought someone was stalking you."

"Because he blames himself for his fiancée's

murder, that if he'd taken care of her, he'd have been able to prevent it. There again, it's the man thing. They think they're responsible for protecting their women. They should remember they're human first, then men."

"That's profound. Can I put that on my thought-of-the-day calendar?"

"You have my permission. By the way, how are things with you and Sam?"

Darcy actually blushed. "Never been better." She gave Rebecca a sly smile. "I think he's going to give me a ring for Christmas."

Rebecca's mouth fell open. She reached out to grab Darcy's hand. "Oh, Darce, I'm so happy for you."

"He hasn't said so for sure, but he's sure hinted at it, and I'm pretty sure."

"And you're going to say 'yes'?"

"Of course. I'd marry him by Thanksgiving, if he asked."

"Your mother would have a conniption if you didn't give her enough time to plan a big church wedding."

"You're right about that." Darcy sipped her tea, her features taking on a serious look. "Who might want to harm you? I suppose everyone in a high-power job has somebody who wants to do them in. Have you rubbed someone the wrong way?"

"I thought about this guy named Moran—my predecessor. They demoted him for insulting a customer and sent him to Bio, but I don't know how he could've gotten ahold of that package of spiders."

Darcy made a face. "Sent to Bio. Oh, that sounds horrible, like something next to purgatory."

In the middle of taking a sip, Rebecca spewed her tea in the middle of a laugh. "Now look what you made me do." She sopped up the mess with her napkin.

"Sorry, I didn't mean to strangle you," Darcy said, not sounding the least bit sorry. "How about Cindy Wasselman? She had her eye on Ben. Might be jealous."

"Cindy Wasselman? From church? True, she's never been friendly toward me for some reason, but that's extreme."

"She a driver for a postal service."

"Is she? I didn't know that. But that's silly. Cindy wouldn't go to that extreme over a man."

"It wouldn't take much to deliver the package to the wrong address. If she were discovered, she could just say it was a mistake."

Rebecca pressed a fresh napkin to her lips. "I suppose I could trace the name of the delivery man—or woman." She shook her head. "No, that's plain silly, and I'm going to drop the whole thing. As I said, it was just a coincidence."

Darcy got up and began clearing the table. "Maybe, but I say you should give Ben a chance. He might be the one, little boy and all."

"I'll keep it in mind."

She had a feeling Ben Lucas was going to be hard to keep off her mind.

Chapter 7

Yea though I walk through the valley of the shadow of death, I will fear no evil; for You are with me; Your rod and Your staff, they comfort me. -Psalm 23:4

I have no trouble distinguishing the true from false in the natural world. Why can't I see the obvious in the spiritual? -Rebecca Atkins

Conference meetings kept Rebecca glued to the office the next several days. Ben sent her a text, inviting her to lunch, but she had to decline. Since she sat on the panel taking overseas calls, lunch was called in. If she'd remembered Darcy had a date tonight, she would have invited Ben to dinner. By the time the conference ended, he would have gone home, and she wouldn't ask him to return to the city. Besides, he had to pick up Jamie from the sitter.

Probably just as well. Nothing would scare him off better than her cooking.

She got a sandwich and fries from the corner diner. After changing into lounge pants, she turned on background music and went over her notes from today's conference until her eyes started burning.

Enough of that. Time to embrace the best part of the night. Taking a shower, getting into her pajamas and reading. No disruptions, no demands, just perfect peace. Before she headed to the bathroom, she flopped on the curved sofa of the living area. It faced the floor to ceiling windows and Rebecca loved viewing the night skyline.

This was the best perk of her new job. Making enough to afford a luxury apartment in the heart of the city.

Most nights she just sat here and enjoyed the view, meditating and praying, but not tonight. Her thoughts kept drifting back to Ben. He was seriously concerned for her. Something deep inside the womanly side of her liked that. But Ben had too much baggage, she reminded herself...and a son. She simply couldn't imagine being a mother.

If only she could be a mother like hers had been. But what an unhappy life Mom had had, all because of Dad's abuse. Running from city to town to city. He always found them until the day he'd died of cirrhosis of the liver from a lifetime of drinking.

Ben certainly wasn't an alcoholic, but he had problems all the same, problems she didn't want to deal with. His experience with his fianceé had left him bruised emotionally. Too cautious. Too protective. He might smother her.

At least he was a Christian. Jason wasn't even that, as she'd found out almost too late. Her father had been a Christian, too, when he'd married Mom, or so Mom had thought, before he took to drinking. Even before that, he'd been legalistic, ruled by the law instead of love. That's why she looked with suspicion on the men in her Sunday School class and shied away from forming a relationship with any of them.

Until Ben.

The city was beautiful tonight. How would she like living in the suburbs, in Haven? With Ben and Jamie.

Why even think about it?

The romance she'd been reading lay on the table calling her. Time for a bath. Jammies.

She made her way to the bathroom and took her earrings out. Get the water running before undressing. She pulled the shower curtains back and froze in terror—

For a moment she couldn't move. With heart pounding, breaths coming in and out, she stared at spiders covering the shower stall. Running all along the wall, each bearing a red dot. Black widows. What she saw was impossible. She had to get out of here. Now.

She stumbled to the door and ran back through the living area, across to the opposite wall, her eyes fixed on the bottom of the door in case one of the demons crawled out.

Please God, not a panic attack. Help me.

Rebecca didn't know how long she stuck to the wall before managing to grapple for her cell in her jeans pocket.

With shaking hands, she swiped Darcy's number, then let her head fall against the wall, sending up a prayer that Darcy had returned from her dinner date.

As she waited for her friend to answer, another horror hit her. Black widows didn't just show up like that. They were solitary spiders, weren't they? They wouldn't appear in mass.

Unless someone planted them.

"Hello."

"Darcccy." Rebecca realized she shivered. "Are you home?"

"Sam just dropped me off. What's up?"

"Come up here now, please."

"Rebecca, what's wrong?"

"Come...now...please."

"I am on my way, Rebecca. Stay on the phone. What happened?"

"Yooou'll see."

Rebecca slid along the wall to the front door and

unlocked it for Darcy. She darted back to her far corner, unable to get in enough air. That familiar feeling of suffocating assailed her.

No, don't hyperventilate. Hold your breath. Darcy's coming.

In the distance she heard the elevator. What if it wasn't Darcy? What if it was *him*? Rebecca twisted her head just far enough to see down the hall. Her breathing slowed a bit as Darcy flung open the door and pounded the polished hardwood.

"Rebecca, what happened, honey? You're white as a sheet."

"Spiders in the bathroom." Rebecca forced her breathing to slow.

"Come show me."

"No, no." Her breathing sped up.

"All right. Try to calm yourself, Becca. Spiders can't hurt you."

Darcy knew about her phobia but had never seen a demonstration. "They're black widows, Darcy, dozens of them." Dozens was probably an exaggeration, but there were a lot.

Patting her cheeks smartly, Darcy nodded. "I know...you're afraid of spiders. But I'm not."

"No, Darcy." Rebecca grabbed her friend in a vise grip. "You don't understand. Someone had to put them in there. He may still be around here."

"He? Who?"

"I don't know." She shook her head. "Ben was right. Someone is stalking me, using spiders to torture me. I can't go back in there, Darcy. If you'll let me, I'll sleep on your sofa tonight."

"Sure, if you'll sleep better. Don't panic." Darcy's tone said she wasn't convinced. "Where are your nerve pills?"

"In the bathroom, but they might be expired by now." She hadn't had to take anything for anxiety in a long time.

"Okay. I'll get your toothbrush." Darcy forestalled Rebecca's raised hand. "Then we'll both go back to my apartment and figure what to do in the morning."

"Darcy..." Rebecca tried to hold onto Darcy, but she pulled away before Rebecca could stop her and, plucking a magazine from the coffee table, marched to the bathroom.

Rebecca jumped when the smack of rolled magazine striking porcelain reached her ears—two, three, a dozen times. Then silence. After several seconds, a toilet flushing sounded, and Darcy ducked back out.

"You sure were right. They were spiders, but they're gone now. I grabbed your toothbrush. Let's go."

It helped to be with Darcy and in her apartment, but Rebecca couldn't get it out of her mind that those spiders were in the same building, just a floor above. But at least there was no mad man lurking in the shadows here. She hoped.

Darcy double locked the door, insisted Rebecca

drink some chamomile tea, and prayed with her.

The sleeper sofa was a marvel, operated by remote control and a six-inch mattress. It was quite comfortable, but Rebecca was certain she wouldn't sleep a minute. It was hard enough to keep her eyes closed. She gazed out the window and was comforted by the fact they were on the twenty-first floor.

Slowly her heart rate returned to normal and the tea made her drowsy. Before she knew it, Rebecca drifted into the oblivion of dreamless sleep.

Chapter 8

Give us help from trouble, for the help of man is useless. Through God we will do valiantly. For it is He who shall tread down our enemies. -Psalm 60:11-12

If a man can't be an instrument of God to help the defenseless, what good is he? -Ben Lucas

"Better eat up, buddy. The bus will be here in a minute." Ben wet a dishcloth and wiped the counter, working around Jamie. The little boy brought another spoonful of bran cereal mixed with his favorite sugared variety.

Adding a bit of the sweet cereal was a concession Ben allowed to coax Jamie to eat. He'd already drunk his juice.

"I'm glad it's Friday. Are you going to see Miss Rebecca again?"

Busy stacking dishes in the dishwasher, Ben straightened, surprised at the question. Jamie hadn't mentioned Rebecca all week. He'd wanted to call her for a date but held back. Something in the way she acted during their walk made him think she'd say no.

"I don't know. You wouldn't have a problem with that, would you?"

"No, I like her. She understands me and doesn't talk to me like I'm a little kid." Jamie jumped down off his stool and brought his cereal bowl to the dishwasher. "Mazy's dad goes out with a lady. Mazy says he may marry her."

Mazy was one of Jamie's classmates whose mother had died several years ago. "That's good, isn't it? Mazy may get a new mother."

"Yes, she's excited. Are you going to get me a new mother?"

Ben had given no thought to how to answer that question. He put a hand on Jamie's shoulder. "I hope so, but it's too soon to say who that'll be. We need to think about it."

"I already do, and I've been praying you'll go out with Miss Rebecca again."

Before Ben could think of a reply, a horn sounded. "The bus." He made wide strides to the chair where

Jamie's book bag lay and fitted it over the boy's arms. With a hug, he opened the door, and Jamie ran to the yellow bus just driving up at the end of the drive.

He'd taken Jamie to school for a while after Kelly's death, but he had to ride the bus home and get off with the Yancy children who lived next door, so it made sense for him to start taking the bus in the morning.

As he turned to finish cleaning up the kitchen, his phone chirped. Who could be calling at this time of the morning? He instantly thought of his mother. His dad had taken a tumble a couple of weeks ago, but as far as Ben knew, he was doing well. "Hello."

Her voice came through frantic. "Ben, you were right. Someone is stalking me."

"Rebecca, what happened?"

"I found a mass of black widow spiders in my shower stall last night."

"How could anyone get in? Have you called the police?"

"The police? No, I called security and management. They're up there investigating now."

"Up there? Where are you?"

"I'm with Darcy. I couldn't sleep in my apartment last night."

No, he didn't suppose so. "I'll stop by. I want to hear what they found out, but I think you should report this to the police. Obviously, if the spiders were planted, someone had to have been in your apartment."

"Obviously. You don't have to stop by. I'll make you

late for work." Her breathless tone revealed the state of her mind more than her words. "Darcy went up and got my clothes. Would you believe, I've shaken them and turned them inside out five times and still don't have the nerve to dress."

It was suddenly urgent that he see her, assure himself she was all right. "Listen. Go ahead and get ready for work. I'll pick you up in..." he glanced at the wall clock, "about twenty minutes. Besides, it's on my way." And he didn't want her driving in.

"I'll be all right."

"It'll give us a chance to talk on the way."

"Ben, the Lowell building is just three blocks over. I usually just walk."

He let his head fall back, having forgotten that. "So it will take longer driving. We'll have more time to talk. I'll pick you up out front to save time."

Her soft laughter told him he'd won her over. "Okay. I'll see you in twenty minutes."

In fifteen minutes, Ben drove into the apartment building's front drive. Rebecca was standing outside the main entrance doors. She opened the passenger door, hopped in, and clicked the seatbelt. "I like a man who's ahead of time." Her light tone clashed with the terrified woman he'd heard on the phone.

"So what did the building management say?"

"They won't have a full report until this afternoon, but they assured me the place would be fumigated. From what I heard from the other tenants, they'll have to do the whole building. They're going to put a new lock on my door."

"Does that satisfy you?"

"Of course not. I'm creeped out. I want to know how anyone could get into the building, much less my apartment."

"The culprit might live in the building." He stopped at the red light and caught her startled expression. Apparently, she hadn't considered that.

"What am I going to do?"

"You need to come up with a list of suspects and report it to the police, even if they brush it off."

"What good will that do? The police won't take action without evidence. I don't even know who's doing this. I have no enemies."

"Did your former boyfriend have a key?" He hated the implication, but she had to consider every angle.

"Yes, I used to have goldfish, and when I was on business trips, Jason would feed them for me."

"Why not Darcy?"

"She didn't move in until two months ago."

"We need to talk to the doorman. Since he knew Jason, he might have let him in."

"I suppose. We?"

He went through all the reasons why he should be involved and came up empty, except that he felt led to help this woman. "I'd like to help you, Rebecca. You need friends at a time like this...and I know a little about how stalkers operate."

"Thank you, Ben. I can't argue with your perception." He wouldn't argue with her sarcasm.

All too soon he drove into the parking deck at the Lowell building. Rebecca still sat in the passenger seat after he'd gotten out. He didn't think she was inviting his assistance. More likely, she was too deep in thought to realize he'd stopped.

He opened her door and she started. "Try not to worry too much. When I take you home, we'll talk with the doorman and the head of security at your building."

"Fortunately, my job doesn't allow much time for worry." She flashed him a smile. "What about Jamie?"

"The next door neighbor will take care of him until I get home. He gets off the bus at their house. Cheryl is very sweet. She says one more isn't any trouble."

As they rode the elevator, he decided to take a chance. "Jamie asked me if I was going to see you again."

"Well, apparently you have."

"He meant socially."

"Oh." The elevator door slid open at his floor.

"We'll talk later."

He had all day to think of a way to take her mind of spiders and stalkers and give him a chance to get to know her better.

Chapter 9

I say to you, though he will not rise and give to him because he is his friend, yet because of his persistence he will rise and give him as many as he needs. -Luke 11:8

Ben is determined to have a deeper friendship than I may be ready for, but I love his persistence. -Rebecca Atkins

In the office, Rebecca decided the less she said about her private turmoil the better, so she went about her duties as usual. But it was harder than usual to read reports and stay focused. Oddly enough, fear of a potential stalker didn't occupy her thoughts as much as Ben did.

All things work together for good.

Had God allowed this to happen so she and Ben would be thrown together? The workings of God were mysterious.

Ben was going to help her. She hugged that thought all day. But she couldn't just stand on the sidelines like a damsel in distress. She pulled up the personnel roster for Biological Research, thirty names, none of whom she knew except Davidson. After reading each bio, she knew little more than when she started. No one there could possibly hold a grudge against her—except Moran. She finally found the records of his time at Bay.

He'd worked in Bio before, for ten years. In fact, the personal files didn't show any move out of that department. Curious.

She took out her notepad and wrote down the other suspects who might mean her harm.

Jason. He was a snake and an egotist. One who didn't take rejection well. Lyle Moran for sure. He had plenty of reason to hate her, illogical reason and logical. She even listed Cindy Wasselman.

There wasn't a shred of evidence linking them to the incidences, not anything she could take to the police anyway.

Ben called her twice, both times she was preoccupied with conferences. She'd call him back before quitting time, which was fast approaching.

She hadn't eaten lunch. Her leftover lunch was still

sitting in her refrigerator at home. Now her stomach rumbled in protest. "Margaret, I'm going to the café and get a Danish and coffee."

"Can I get it for you, Rebecca?"

"No, I need to stretch." She grabbed her coin purse and made for the door. "If Ben calls, tell him I'll call him as soon as I return. Anyone else, tell them I'm out for the day."

The little café was situated across from the elevators and they'd be closing soon. In fact, the clerk was wiping down the counters when she strode up. "Do you have a Danish left?"

"Yes, ma'am, apple and cheese."

"I'll take an apple and a small coffee with cream." She extracted the exact amount as the clerk filled her order.

"Good afternoon, Ms. Atkins."

She jerked around to see a medium built, curly brown-haired man who looked somewhat familiar. But maybe that was because he looked like a young Garfunkel. "Good afternoon. Did you miss lunch, too?"

He smiled affably. "No, I like a snack in the afternoon." He laughed. "In the morning and night, if I'm honest." He turned his attention to the clerk. "I'll take a honeybun and coffee."

"I'm afraid I don't know everyone on this floor, but you look familiar." She'd probably recognize his name from the profiles she'd read, but she wouldn't tell him that.

"I work for Harold Davidson, Ms. Atkins. Well, directly under Lyle Moran. I'm Derek Gammon." He turned back to the clerk. "That reminds me, Lyle asked me to get him some mint gum, any brand you have." He shifted his attention back to Rebecca. "We interviewed for the research chief's job, Miss Atkins. By the way, congratulations belatedly."

"Thank you." She took her pastry and coffee and gave Gammon a smile. "I remember. I'm glad you decided to take another job here at Bay." She started to turn away when he stopped her.

"My brother is head of maintenance at your apartment building. He told me about the spider scare you had last night."

"Oh, did he say what they're doing about it?"

"They're getting rid of the spiders, no worry about that. Tad told me they could've come from anywhere. Someone might have a kid somewhere in the building who collects spiders and let them loose. They could've gotten into the drain pipes and hatched out in your pipes."

She tried to wrap that theory around her brain. Was this possibly just another weird coincidence? Not likely. "Well, so long as they're gotten rid of them." No need to let strangers know about her phobia. "I'll be seeing you around, Mr. Gammon."

When Rebecca got back to her office, she keyed in Derek Gammon to bring up more details from his file. Wow. He held an MIT master's and had seven years with a New York firm. How did she win out over him? She made a note to ask Dr. Breckenridge that very question when she saw him. At any rate, Gammon worked with plants, not venomous creatures.

She pressed in Ben's number. "Hi, sorry I missed you earlier."

"That's all right. I just wanted to check on how you were doing today."

"Fine. I feel safe enough here. It's going home that has me edgy."

She wished he'd say she was being silly, but a cautious note entered his voice. "I know, but we'll get to the bottom of it. It's a bad feeling to have your home being violated."

That was exactly what she'd felt, like her space had been violated. "This thing has stolen my peace, and I'm really going to have a hard time going back into my own home."

"I'll go up with you and check it out."

"Thank you. As silly as that sounds, I appreciate it."

On the way home, Rebecca related what Gammon had told her about the maintenance man's theory. Ben didn't think much of it. "Anything's possible, I suppose, but I've found the odds of something happening twice is astonishing, three times, near impossible. We'll talk to the maintenance man as well."

And they did. They questioned the maintenance man, the head of security, and the doorman who couldn't recall seeing Jason in months.

Ben walked her to her apartment. They checked every nook and cranny together. All was as it should be, no evidence of spiders or any pests, human or animal.

They stood looking out the window for a long time. Dusk had descended and the city's lights shown—a beautiful, peaceful sight. She felt safe with Ben beside her, but he had to leave.

With a deep sigh he faced her. "I've got to get going. Are you going to be all right?"

"I think so. Thank you for coming."

"No need for thanks. Do you mind if we pray about it?"

"I wish you would."

He took both her hands. "Heavenly Father, I pray for your peace for Rebecca. Blanket her with your protection. Help her to look upon spiders as one of Your creations to bring order to nature. We know all fear comes from Satan, and we ask you, Father, to bind him in Jesus's name. Bring that peace that defies understanding to this apartment. Return that peace to Rebecca, and we give You all the glory. Amen."

Ben squeezed her hands and for the moment, peace did descend upon her. She walked him to the door. Still he seemed loathe to leave. "There's a carnival in Haven. Tomorrow's the last day so I've promised Jamie I'd take him. Would you come with us? Unless you have other plans." A look of boyish uncertainty crossed his face.

Tomorrow was Saturday. "I have no plans and I'd love to go to the carnival."

Ben grinned. "Good. We'll pick you up at five. We'll have that rich carnival food and let Jamie ride until he gets sick."

"What? I don't get to ride?"

He laughed. "Sure, though most of the rides are for no taller than this." He held his hand chest high.

"I'll look forward to it, and thank you again for soothing my nerves, especially for the prayer."

"We'll keep praying and investigating, I promise you that."

He held onto the door knob, then dipped his head. His kiss surprised her, and a good thing it did. If she'd had time to think about it, she might have clung to him.

"Goodnight, Rebecca." He was gone so quickly she suspected he'd realized the kiss shouldn't linger.

Chapter 10

My brethren, count it all joy when you fall into various trials, knowing that the testing of your faith produces patience. But let patience have its perfect work, that you may be perfect and complete, lacking nothing. -James 1:2-4

I thought the love of a woman would be a long time coming after Kelly, but here I am growing impatient. -Ben Lucas

It probably wasn't the best idea to wait until the last day to take Jamie to the carnival. The venues and rides were crowded. Ben and Rebecca held Jamie's hands walking fast from the food concessions. Not that they feared losing him—just to keep up with him.

They took a right into the kiddy rides area. "Aw, I'm too old for the baby rides," Jamie pouted.

Rebecca pulled him in line. "If you go on the flying elephants with me, I'll go on one of the big rides with you."

Ben tore off the required tickets and handed them to Rebecca. She smiled. "You're not going with us?"

"I don't think I'd fit, but have fun."

Ben watched Jamie cling to Rebecca. In spite of his protests, he had a lot of baby still in him. It had been a rough year for him. Jamie had trouble opening up to people, and Ben was surprised his son had connected so quickly with Rebecca.

When he'd first met her, he'd seen the epitome of the high-class career woman. No way would he have imagined she'd take up time with a child and apparently enjoy it. There was more to Rebecca than met the eye. Yet there was a lot for the eye as well. With her honey-tipped dark hair flying in the wind and wide grin revealing perfect teeth, she brought a new feeling to Ben. An attraction he'd not thought possible.

It bothered him his image of Kelly was fading.

"Hello, Ben."

He turned to find Cindy Wasselman holding the hand of a toddler. "Hello, Cindy. Is this little princess yours?" He knew Cindy had two young children but had never paid much attention at church. He did recall seeing the strawberry blonde, cherubic-looking girl in the nursery.

"This is Betsy. Her brother, Robbie, is standing in line for the bumper cars. They scare Betsy. I suppose you're here with Jamie?"

"I am." Ben pointed. "That's him in the yellow elephant, you might recognize the lady with him."

"Rebecca Atkins." The scowl on Cindy's face said a lot. She smiled quickly. "She's done a lot for the Sunday School class. I guess it takes an ambitious woman to get things done."

"She is that, all right."

"My mother lives in her apartment building. She had to spend the day at my place since Rebecca had the whole building fumigated. All over finding a spider. Can you imagine?"

"It was numerous spiders and venomous ones, at that. You should be glad they didn't get in your mother's apartment."

Cindy shrugged. "I didn't know you and Rebecca were dating."

"We've only been out a couple of times." On official dates anyway.

This seemed to please Cindy. "I shouldn't say anything, but you should be careful. Some people aren't the fine Christians they seem to be. Rebecca is very pretty, as well as ambitious."

"Nothing wrong with that." What was she getting at? Whatever it was, he didn't want to find out. "So what grade is Robbie in this year?"

"Third." The ride was coming to an end and Cindy made to go. Unexpectedly, she grabbed Ben's arm. "There's a reason she got that director's job. She knew Dr. Breckenridge very well, if you know what I mean." She stalked away before he could reply, which he wouldn't have done anyway. Feeding gossip was as bad as spreading it.

"Was that Cindy Wasselman?" Rebecca asked as she and Jamie came up.

"Yeah, she's here with her kids."

"That's a cute little girl she has. I really feel sorry for her trying to make a living by herself. Our class ought to do something for her and the kids for Thanksgiving and Christmas."

"Come on, Miss Becca. You promised." Jamie tugged her hand.

She laughed back at Ben and skipped along with Jamie, who was tearing his way to the Pirate's Ship, one of the big rides that swung one hundred and eighty degrees like a giant sew-saw. Since there was plenty of room, Ben rode with them. How could a woman who went into a panic attack over a half-inch spider throw up her hands as they were tossed almost upside down?

After Jamie and Rebecca rode the roller coaster, they all went on the Ferris wheel. She sat in the middle this time, and when it stopped with them at the top, she sent him a sly smile. "Afraid of heights?"

"Not afraid exactly, but I am reminded of the law of gravity."

"I learned something about fear the other night."

"Oh, what?"

"You have to face it head on—not daring, of course—but trusting in God through it all."

"You're right about that."

"I'm not ready to face spiders yet, but I fortified myself with the scriptures. Do you know how many times "fear not" is mentioned in the Bible?"

"How many?"

"I don't know. I was asking you." She laughed and linked her arm through his as they came down the ride's ramp.

"Well, I don't know that, but I do know perfect love casts out fear." They shared a glance, so brief he almost missed it. But in that moment, he knew he wanted to get to know Rebecca Atkins much better. More than that. He wanted her a permanent part of his and Jamie's lives.

"I'm hungry." Jamie announced as they left the Ferris wheel.

"So am I." Rebecca took Jamie's hand and hooked Ben's with her other arm. "Nothing tastes better on a perfect fall day than carnival food."

As they walked to the nearest concessions, Ben decided to take a chance. "Week after next is Thanksgiving. Jamie and I are going up to Michigan. My folks have a place on the lake. How would you like to go with us?" It might be short notice for a woman who had a harried life, but nothing ventured, nothing gained.

"Are you from Michigan?"

"Originally, yes. I'd like to show you my boyhood home."

"Will there be snow?"

He let his hopes soar. It was getting more important that she say yes. "It has snowed by Thanksgiving, but I don't think there's any on the ground now. But who knows? It can turn frigid overnight."

"I wish I could. Truth is, I was going to help Darcy cook for the homeless shelter. Actually, she'll be cooking. I'll be serving."

His hopes evaporated in a whiff of disappointment. How could one argue with plans as noble as that?

"Maybe another time."

They walked up to the corndog stand. After that, they ate funnel cakes. If this didn't give him indigestion, nothing would.

"Can I play some games, Dad?"

"We've used up the ride tickets, but I think we can spare ten dollars for games—and no goldfish." Ben had made the mistake of letting Jamie win a goldfish at the fair. It had died the next day.

Jamie picked up ducks, threw rings on bottles, and tossed a basketball until he had a pocketful of useless junk. He wanted to shoot for a big prize. Naturally the burly man hawking the game egged him on.

"All right, buddy, but it costs two dollars. That's all we have left. One chance, that's it."

Naturally, Jamie missed. "Why don't you try, Ben?" Rebecca was no help.

"Please, Dad. I want the panda."

Ben took out another two dollars and selected a gun. He had to hit the bell three times for a panda. He worked with the sight until the hawker complained. "Gonna show us what you got tonight?"

Ben closed one eye and fired. Ding. He had the sights right. The bell dinged two more times, much to the hawker's displeasure, his enthusiasm gone as he unhooked the big stuffed panda bear and handed it to Jamie. Rebecca clapped her hands, and Ben had the foolish notion to go again to win her a panda. But he wasn't a teenager trying to impress a girl, and it was getting late.

Without giving it much thought, he slipped his arm around Rebecca's waist as they strode to the parking lot. Jamie caught her hand on the other side, hugging the stuffed toy to his chest.

It would be easy to get used to this—a real family.

As they found Ben's truck, a red convertible passed them and the woman in the passenger's side waved. Cindy Wasselman. Ben sensed Rebecca tense. "What is it?"

"That man with Cindy."

Busy getting Jamie locked into his car seat, Ben sent a questioning glance over his shoulder. "Yeah?"

"Unless I'm greatly mistaken, it was Jason."

He straightened and studied Rebecca's features. Was she jealous? Did she still have feelings for Jason?

She shrugged and got into the passenger's side. When he belted into the driver's seat, she dove into her handbag. "Would you believe I haven't checked my messages all day?"

"Sounds good to me. Everybody needs a break from the machines now and then."

She laughed and swiped her phone. Then her face turned pale.

"Something wrong?"

She held the phone up, screen facing him. He read the text.

I'm watching you.

He took her hand resting on her knee. "I assume you don't recognize this number."

"No."

"We're going to get it traced."

"What if the police won't do that?"

"I know someone who will."

Chapter 11

He who despises his neighbor sins; but he who has mercy on the poor, happy is he. - Proverbs 14:21

Most men want to impress me by showing me a good time. I've never known one who will sacrifice his own plans for the sake of others. – Rebecca Atkins

Rebecca dropped her handbag on the sofa and gazed out the windows at the street below. The peace she'd found in Sunday School was shattered by the visit to the Police Precinct. The young officer who took her statement was nice, but she got the feeling he was laughing behind her back. If Ben hadn't insisted they take her charges seriously, she doubted they'd even promise to trace the phone number that left that cryptic note. They'd have dismissed her outright.

That was new to her. She usually got respect in any situation. But in all other situations she made sure she had her facts straight and could back up anything she said. She couldn't make any sense of what was happening now.

Darcy had a date with Sam so Rebecca had the entire evening to herself. She might as well catch up on some work. After staring at the computer screen for ten minutes she gave up.

Ben had asked her for their first just-the-two-of-them date, a play at the local high school. The daughter of one of Ben's co-workers was in the play, and he'd bought a ticket weeks before.

He wanted her to spend Thanksgiving with his family. She wished that were possible. Not only did she want to spend time with Ben and meet his family, she desperately wanted to get out of town, away from the reach of whoever pursued her.

Why would anyone want to pursue her? But when did a madman or woman need an excuse?

Her phone sounded an incoming text. Since yesterday, she feared even looking, but she did.

She breathed easier when she saw it came from Ben. *I have news. Give me a call when you have time.*

Had the police called him? She went into contacts

and tapped his number and he answered almost immediately. "What's the news?" She had a bad habit of being too abrupt, but he already understood her. Why he did, she didn't know, but he would.

"You were sitting on ready." He laughed.

"Don't keep me in suspense."

"I had a long talk with my mom and dad this afternoon."

How could that be news? Fortunately, she had the presence of mind to be polite. "How are they?"

"Great. Dad had an accident a few weeks ago, but he's almost recovered. Anyway, I told them about you, and they really want to meet you. If Jamie and I stay until late Thanksgiving Day, I could help out at the soup kitchen along with you and Darcy, then we can all go to Michigan."

She took too long to digest what he was saying and he went on, "Cheryl will take care of Jamie." He chuckled again. "Jamie will get two thanksgiving dinners."

"That's wonderful, Ben, we'd love to have your help at the homeless shelter, but I wouldn't want you to make your parents hold Thanksgiving dinner for my sake." She yawned, giving away the fact she hadn't slept well last night. But she didn't want him to take it for boredom so she forced a bright note to her voice and added, "Not that I wouldn't enjoy a real sit-down family meal this year and my folks are on a world cruise."

"It won't be any trouble to change mine and Jamie's tickets for late Thanksgiving Day, and I could easily get you one at the same time."

The enthusiasm in his voice told her better than anything that this guy really liked her. He wanted her to meet his parents. That meant— But that was too fast. Still, she really liked him, too, and she needed him in a way she'd never needed a man before. She didn't want to lead him on, though. But he was moving a bit too fast for her.

"Rebecca?"

"I'm still here. I guess you surprised me is all. If it's not too much trouble getting me a ticket, and if you're sure your folks wouldn't mind me barging in, then yes, I'd like to have Thanksgiving with you guys."

"That's great. I'll call the folks back and let them know. You won't be barging in. They'll love to have you—and I will, too."

"Tell them to order snow. If I'm going all the way to Michigan, I want to see some."

"Let's hope. So what's the set-up for cooking for the homeless?"

"I'll be serving, and we'd love to have you. We can always use another server. You just dip a serving in the plate as the people come down the line. But be prepared for a shock at who shows up."

"Oh, how so?"

"They're not derelict alcoholics. Most are women and children. It's very sad. I'm just saying—I know you have a compassionate heart, and it's going to get bruised." Knowing how he'd stepped up to help her, she knew he'd have a hard time.

"So I'll want to do more."

"Definitely. I always want to do more. Say, have you heard from the police?"

"No, I assume they'll contact you. Trouble is, they never think something is as urgent as you think it is."

"I suppose so." She tried to think of something else to say, just to keep him on the line. Acting like a teenager. "I guess I should get off the line so you can call your folks. Tell them thanks for the invite."

"Are you okay there by yourself?" Anxiety laced his words.

"Yes, with the new locks, I feel fairly safe. At least I know no one can climb through the windows—one advantage of living in a high-rise."

That brought on that delightful chuckle she enjoyed hearing. "That's right. The other reason I called I contacted a private detective. This is a friend of my lawyer's back in Wisconsin. He wants to talk to you at your place. Will you mind if we drop in tonight after work?"

She brightened. "I'd like that. Come early enough for dinner. Darcy and I are going to make lasagna. Actually, I'm going to follow Darcy's instructions since she's the cook."

"Sounds good. Wish I could, but Tom has a family, and they expect him for dinner each night. He's doing me a favor to come out afterward. Will you be alone after eight?"

She released a deflated sigh. "Yes, that will be fine. Is this detective going to find the creep who's trying to scare me?"

"That's what we hope. He's a no-nonsense type of guy, and good at tracking down the truth as well as creeps. He's hired by Atlanta's top defense lawyers—a real Paul Drake."

"Who?"

Apparently that struck Ben as funny. He laughed again. "You know, Perry Mason's detective. I thought you were into old TV shows."

"No, just old movies, but Perry Mason sounds familiar." She glanced at the pile of reports screaming for attention while she sat here, chatting with Ben like she had all the time in the world. "Oh, I know now. My mom is a huge detective books fan. Earl Stanley Garner, right? She had two rows of his books, along with Agatha Christie and Sherlock Holmes. She says the books are always better than the TV shows or movies."

"That's the way it usually is. Know why? Your imagination isn't as limited as the screen writer."

She wanted to get into a whole new conversation about that, but she was on company time, so she held back as Ben added, "Your mom and mine will get along great. My mom has a whole row of Mary Higgins Clark."

Margaret's hot button flashed. "I have an incoming call, Ben, but I really want to meet Paul Drake."

"His name is Tom Laster, Rebecca, but you call him Paul Drake. He'll get a kick out of that."

She laughed. "All right, I will. Bye for now, Ben."

There wouldn't be much joking tonight, though.

Chapter 12

Anxiety in the heart of man causes depression, but a good word makes it glad. -Proverbs 12:25

I'm blessed to have a friend I can depend on for the truth, even when it's something I'd rather not hear. -Ben Lucas

Tom Laster had gone to the same college as Ben, and they'd shared a dorm their freshman year. Blond and muscular, he gave the appearance of a beachboy, more observant of his classmates than the professors, and Ben wasn't surprised when Tom dropped out in his junior year and teamed up with a former police captain and his son to form the detective agency. Then two years ago, Tom moved to Atlanta and set up his own agency.

Ben pulled into a parking slot in visitor parking at Rebecca's apartment building. Up until now, Tom had been telling Ben about his last camping trip along the Altamaha River.

As Ben walked around the car, Tom was taking his measure of the place. "There isn't many visitor parking slots available. Must be hard to find a place during business hours."

"Near impossible."

"Where is the resident parking? How many decks?"

"No decks. It's all underground," Ben replied, wondering how that was significant.

They showed their credentials at the security desk. "I'm thinking of getting a place here. Do you know if security extends to the parking garage?" Tom asked the bored guard. Ben turned away to keep from showing a grin. When did Tom learn to lie so convincingly?

"The entrance from the garage is controlled by card key."

"Thank you," Tom said.

"What was that all about?" Ben asked as they rode up in the elevator.

"Just getting the lay of the land. Impossible to know who left the plastic spider on her car. Probably impossible to know who left the spiders on her desk at work." They exited the elevator. "Even if the police can trace that text, it's unlikely they'll tell us."

Ben gestured toward the left. "But whoever left those spiders in her bathroom had to have gotten in this building."

"Exactly, and I've found building security is a lot more forthcoming than the police. They'd notice any strangers. But that won't help if the culprit is a resident."

Rebecca opened the door immediately. Dressed in ivory silk shirt and navy pants, her hair held up with a silver clip, she was stunning. After introductions, she and Tom shook hands. Ben was grateful Tom was a happily married man, since he was a handsome man and had that aura of mystic women loved.

"Would you gentlemen like a drink? I have several brands of soft drink and coffee. Nothing stronger. Sorry."

"No thank you, Ms. Atkins," Tom said.

"Please, call me Rebecca. I'd feel more comfortable if we kept it informal. We can sit over here." She moved toward the sofa in front of the tall window wall, the Atlanta skyline lit up behind it.

"If you don't mind, I'd like to look around first." Tom sent a sweeping glance around the apartment.

"Not at all." She sent a relaxed smile to Ben and they sat while Tom went first to her bedroom, then to the bath.

After a couple of minutes, he stuck his head out the door. "Rebecca, would you come here?"

Ben tagged along.

Tom held a gum wrapper. "Do you chew this brand of gum?"

"I don't chew gum at all."

"I found this stuck to the inside of your waste basket. Strange thing is, the sticky substance that held it was only present at that particular place. Kind of like someone glued the paper there." He showed them the wrapper, actually only a part of it. "Looks like someone tried to tear it off, but it was stuck fast. Did you empty the basket between the time you saw the spiders and now?"

"No, but my cleaning lady did. She comes in once a week. Except last week. I'd changed my locks and forgot to give her a key."

"Anyone been in your apartment except her?"

"Ben, of course, and Darcy, my downstairs friend."

"Don't forget the super who sprayed for spiders."

"That's right. Jimmy Leavy. It could have been his wrapper, though I've never seen him chewing gum. Besides, Jimmy is the sweetest thing and a bit mentally challenged. I couldn't believe he'd have anything to do with it."

Tom had been jotting notes on a small pad as she answered.

"Do you know anyone of your acquaintance who chews gum? Someone from work, perhaps."

Rebecca threw back her head giving them a lovely view of the slope of her neck. "No, not that I've noticed.

I don't know a lot of them well, though." A startled look came into those dark blue eyes. "Wait. I remember I was at the concession stand of the lobby café getting a Danish the other day when Mr. Gammon came up. He mentioned he was buying some mint gum for Mr. Moran."

Quiet pressed in, disturbed only by the scratching of Tom's pen as he wrote. He snapped the pad closed. "I'm ready to sit and discuss your suspects now."

Rebecca and Ben sat together on the sofa, while Tom took the adjacent chair. There would be no small talk. No joking. That wasn't Tom's style. "Why do you think Lyle Moran might be stalking you?"

"I don't personally know of anything. I'm assuming he would blame me for his firing." She released a heavy breath. "There are rumors, supposedly put out by Mr. Moran, that I was hired because I'm Dr. Breckenridge's...girlfriend."

"Dr. Breckenridge is the CEO?"

"That's right."

"And your immediate supervisor?" When she nodded, he asked another question. "Who told you these rumors?"

She moved her head from one side to the other, sliding Ben a glance. "I don't remember who mentioned it first. It was just water cooler talk that I wasn't supposed to hear."

"Is Dr. Breckenridge aware of these rumors?"

She released a short laugh. "I doubt it. No one would have dared mention something like that to him."

"But for all you know, someone did. Maybe someone told Mrs. Breckenridge. I assume he's married."

Color drained from her face. "Surely no one would have done that."

"Maybe you should talk to Dr. Breckenridge about this—and the sooner, the better."

Ben took her hand. "That would be embarrassing for Rebecca, and might stir up trouble."

Tom nodded. "Sometimes you have to stir up trouble to flush out the guilty." He tapped his pen against the pad. "I don't know how you handle it, Ms. Atkins, but you'll have to explain to Breckenridge what's been happening. If for no other reason, he needs to know if someone in his company may be unhinged."

"A mad scientist?" Rebecca tried to laugh that off.

"A jealous person, whether a scientist or not, we can't tell yet."

"Then you don't think it's Jason? He knew about her spider phobia, as far as we know."

"The ex-boyfriend? Not likely from what I've gathered. It's typical to flaunt a new girlfriend in front of Ms. Atkins, but he didn't have access to her apartment."

"Yes, he did," Rebecca said. "When we were dating, I let him have a key to feed my goldfish while I was on a business trip. I forgot to get it back."

"A good thing you've had your keys changed now," Ben said.

"Except security didn't find him entering the building. I'm still going to check the camera at the entrance from the garage."

Ben didn't think he was giving Jason enough suspicion. Then he recalled his new girlfriend. "And speaking of jealousy. Cindy Wasselman tried to tell me those nasty rumors about you while we were at the carnival." Ben hadn't meant to mention that, knowing it would upset Rebecca, but both she and Tom needed to know.

"And she was at the site when we were fixing Mr. Simmons's house," Rebecca added.

Tom took another several minutes to record notes before getting to his feet. Rebecca and Ben followed him to the door. "It'll take a few days to check this out. In the meantime, stay alert. And it's imperative that you confide in Dr. Breckenridge."

"You think Rebecca is in real danger?"

"For certain. Whoever this is took a great deal of trouble to terrorize her with the spiders. Now he, or she, has changed tactics. It could be he's tired of playing games and ready to attack."

Chapter 13

So it was, when the king saw Queen Esther standing in the court, and the king held out to Esther the golden scepter that was in his hand. Then Esther went near and touched the top of the scepter. -Esther 5:2

Queen Esther was not the last woman believed to receive favors in the court because of her looks. - Rebecca Atkins

Tom Laster left Rebecca more on edge than ever. Until now, she'd tried to dismiss everything as Ben's overreaction. The detective's assessment of the situation scared her. Now, she'd be looking over her shoulder at every turn.

Ben had left with Tom, and she'd wanted to cling to him as tightly as a mountain climber clings to a crevice in the rock, afraid to go any further, but having to. He could sense it too. At the door, he'd brushed her hair back and kissed her—not a passionate kiss. One meant to reassure.

She found everyone going through the normal routine at work the next morning. No surprise packages. A full calendar awaited her, but there was one appointment she'd have to work in. After Margaret had brought her coffee, following up with the usual rundown of the day, she said, "Will you see when Dr. Breckenridge can see me? There's a matter of importance I have to discuss with him."

Margaret looked surprised. Rebecca had never asked for an appointment before, although she'd been called into Dr. Breckenridge's office several times since taking her new position.

Assuming he was even in today, it was unlikely he'd give her an appointment until later in the day, so Rebecca sipped her coffee as she went through the mail. Margaret surprised her by popping back in immediately.

"Dr. Breckenridge can see you now."

Her pulse kicked up. She'd expected to have more time to gather her thoughts. How did one tell her boss they were an item of gossip? But one didn't keep Dr. Breckenridge waiting. "Thank you, Margaret. I'm on my way."

The executive office took up the entire suite above the main floor, complete with all the amenities you'd expect of the company's CEO. She'd been in here often enough to get the lay of the place, though it had scared her silly during that first initial interview.

Dr. Breckenridge's secretary ushered her directly into his private office.

He stood in front of the window and turned as she entered. "Good morning, Rebecca, please have a seat. Have you had your coffee?"

"Yes, sir, thank you." She sank into the plush butter leather chair offered. "I won't take up much of your time."

Dr. Breckenridge took his chair behind his massive desk. A tall, imposing man with graying temples, he smiled affably. He was still handsome, though he must be at least sixty. "How is the R-35 project going?"

The problem at hand occupied her thoughts so completely, she had to think a moment to remember what the R-35 project was. She relaxed. "Very well. I had to reassign Jenkins and Thames. They were at loggerheads over the test schedule."

"I heard that. A very good move. Both are fine chemists, but stubborn."

"That they are."

"So what can I help you with this morning?"

She stared at her hands, fidgeting in her lap, and drew in a fortifying breath. "Dr. Breckenridge, this is difficult for me to say, but I feel I must because you have a right to know."

He leaned forward, propping his elbows on his desk. "Sounds serious."

"It might be. I knew when you placed me in this job it would raise eyebrows since I'm young without a lengthy resume, but the rumor circulating took me by surprise."

"There are always those who feel they could have made a better decision than me."

She met his gaze and found him smiling, no doubt to encourage her to spit it out. "They are saying you gave me this job because...because we were...romantically involved."

Dr. Breckenridge chuckled. "That might have surprised you, Rebecca, but not me. Every time I hire an attractive young woman, those rumors spring up."

"But what if your wife should hear about it?"

He dropped his hands on the desk and threaded his fingers. "Caroline and I have the type of relationship that's built on complete trust, and neither of us have ever been betrayed. Don't get married before you find someone like that, Rebecca."

A vision of Ben flashed through her mind. He was the first man she felt she could trust like that. She smiled. "Don't worry about that. I wouldn't. I shouldn't have even brought it up, but...well...I didn't want it to cause problems."

"No problem at all. Just ignore such things, and they'll die a natural death, sooner than you think. I'm not going to deny that you will have trouble gaining the respect of some of our people, but I have no doubt you will."

"Thank you, Dr. Breckenridge. I'd better get back to work."

"Not at all. Anytime—my office is open."

She strode to the door and rested her hand on the knob when curiosity made her stop. Dr. Breckenridge was so easy to talk to, why not ask what really bothered her. "May I ask one question before I leave?"

"Certainly."

"Why did you hire me when there were candidates so much more qualified?"

His smile died. "What makes you think they were more qualified?"

"I mean on paper, at least. I've looked over the resumes, and Derek Gammon for example, went to better colleges and has several more years of experience than I do."

He gestured for her to return. "You would agree scientists are a different breed of employee?"

"Definitely."

"For the most part, they are atheists. I say for the most part because I don't think anyone can really deny the existence of God. But they are trained to think that way and conditioned to think that's smart."

"Sort of like Pavlov's dog."

He laughed, a jolly rolling laugh. "They wouldn't appreciate the analogy, but yes, exactly like that. If they give the answer they think their colleagues expect of an intelligent person, they think they'll be rewarded. If not, they'll be ridiculed. Yes, exactly like Pavlov's dog."

"You are a very intelligent man, sir, and it's an honor to work for you, but you haven't answered my question. Why did you hire me out of so many qualified candidates?"

"Do you recall at the end of your interview, after you'd told me all the things you could do for the company?"

She didn't have to think long. Every moment of the interview played through her mind for days as she'd waited for his decision. "You asked what I could do for my subordinates."

He nodded. "That question usually throws my interviewees for a loop, but you didn't hesitate a moment. You said you'd love them as you did yourself. Not even God asks us for more than that. How could I?"

Tears burned the backs of her eyes. She'd not thought of it like that. "It's true. I know scientists, many are anti-religious, and I understand that part about being ridiculed, but I've yet to find anyone who wouldn't accept love. If a person understands that God is love, he can believe."

"Well stated, Rebecca. I hope I've assured you the rumors don't affect me or my wife at all. Just ignore them."

"I will. Thank you, Dr. Breckenridge. One more question. Why was Lyle Moran's record as research chief expunged?"

Dr. Breckenridge leaned back in his chair and

stared at the ceiling. "You know this is a cut-throat business. Our competitors are snooping around like hungry wolves."

"Yes, sir, I know that."

"Mr. Moran is a brilliant scientist, but he's not a people person. I should have realized that when I placed him in the position. It was only a matter of time before he rubbed someone the wrong way and they took it to the press. He had to go, but I had to find a way to keep him and protect the company at the same time. The only solution was to place another in that position from the beginning. That was you. If the press ever asked you about the matter, you could truthfully tell them you were on your orientation tour and didn't know what happened."

The whole thing reeked of dishonesty, but who was she to question the company's tactics. "Thank you for trusting me enough to tell me, sir."

"I've been well pleased with you, Rebecca. You may not be on the same level as some of our other scientists—yet, anyway—but you are a people person. Just right for your position."

"Thank you, Dr. Breckenridge. I promise to live up to your trust."

When she checked her calls back in her office, she found a text from Ben. Only one word. *Lunch*?

Unfortunately, her schedule only allowed enough time for a sandwich brought in from the diner, but she wanted to get away with Ben. Not at a crowded lunch counter. She tapped his number.

Without a hello, he got to the point. "Can you go?"

"No, I'm sorry. I had a meeting with Dr. Breckenridge so I have to make up the time during lunch. However, I want to take you somewhere that's special to me on Saturday. A place where a miracle happened. Can you get a sitter?"

"As a matter of fact, Jamie is spending the night with his friend. I'm yours all afternoon and evening. Where is this special place?"

"You'll see."

Chapter 14

But I will sing of Your power. Yes, I will sing aloud of Your mercy in the morning; for You have been my defense and refuge in the day of my trouble. -Psalm 59:16

Rebecca took me to her secret refuge today—a place where she has known peace. -Ben Lucas

At Rebecca's direction, Ben drove his four-wheel drive jeep in a southeasterly direction. The terrain would get rough, she'd told him with a sly grin. Outside of Forest Park, they turned onto a county road and left the congested traffic behind. It seemed impossible that just twenty-five miles outside of Atlanta wilderness began.

"Are you taking me to the woods?"

She laughed. "Soon. Why do you think I insisted we come in your jeep?" Shifting forward in her seat, she scanned the left side of the road. "Slow down. Our turn is coming up. I just hope they haven't gated it."

"We're going onto a private drive?"

"It didn't used to be that way, and I don't think it's been posted because it's a short cut to Panola State Park." She strained forward and shook her finger. "There—there's the road."

Ben turned off onto the dirt one-lane road, bouncing over the ruts left by a recent rain. "Did you often come down here?"

"All the time as I was growing up. In the spring, it's full of flowers, and the smell is wonderful. Even in the hottest part of summer, it's cool and refreshing. In the fall, it has the most delightful smell, and so much wildlife to explore. I never came in the winter because that's when the hunters were out."

It would be a good place to hunt. He might ask Tom about it since his friend was an avid outdoorsman.

They had gone about fifteen minutes before suddenly coming upon a clearing dominated by a small lake—a beautiful oasis hidden in the tall pines—as blue as the deepening sky above. And Rebecca Atkins's eyes.

He didn't have to ask if this was the place and cut the engine a dozen yards from the lake's edge.

After taking it all in, he watched Rebecca staring

through the windshield with a dreamy expression, obviously reliving pleasant memories. "Ready to eat?" he asked. They had stopped at the burger joint and brought their dinner, along with drinks.

"No, let's eat out under the trees." She opened her door and grabbed the bag. "You bring the drinks."

She led him into a thicker part of the forest, where a massive oak full of brown and orange leaves stood, and set the bag on the ground, then gathered an armful of pine needles to make a soft seating area.

Ben cleared a level space in the middle to set their drinks and food. They ate in silence, a comfortable silence with no need for words. Only the tweeting of birds mingling with the rustle of the burger wrappings disturbed the quiet.

When finished eating, Ben gathered the trash. "I'm glad you brought me here. It's a beautiful and peaceful place for a picnic."

"My family used to live just down that dirt road, and we came here often because my father liked to fish. My mother would sit under this tree and read."

"Her detective books."

Her lips tipped into a lovely smile. "Right."

"What did you do?"

"I explored. I've always had the naturalist's urge to explore how nature works. And I found bugs and worms for my father to bait his hook. That was one of the few ways I pleased him. It was the only place I remember when he was happy—and not angry or drunk." A world of hurt lay behind those words. She must have felt his

117

stare because she scooted around to meet his gaze. "Do you like to fish?"

"I do. My father used to take me fishing a lot during the summer. I took Jamie a few times...before we moved down here."

"I love all the seasons down here. The thing I like best about these woods are the scents. During the spring and summer, the wildflowers perfume the air. There's a mass of honeysuckle bushes over on the other side of the lake. The fall and winter have their own woodsy scent, full of pine, cedar, and decaying vegetation."

A squirrel chattered his warning overhead and an acorn dropped in Rebecca's lap. She threw it back at him. "You don't own these woods, buddy."

"When's the last time you came out here?"

"With Mama the year before I left for college. We came to pick berries. She wanted to put up some blackberry jelly and make a gooseberry pie for Carl. It must have worked. They got married that Christmas." She got up on her knees. "If I go with you and Jamie to your folks for Thanksgiving, you'll have to go with me to Mama and Carl's for Christmas."

"I'd like to. I'd like to get to know your folks. Where do they live?"

"South of here in Columbus. Carl was in the army, stationed at Fort Benning. He retired two years ago. They travel a lot, but they're always home for Christmas. Carl has two daughters who come with their families for the holidays. He has a son stationed in Germany."

"How do you like Carl?" Ben asked. He knew she hadn't gotten along with her own father.

"He's a fine man from what I can tell, and obviously loves my mother. I was glad she found someone to make her happy."

"I'm sure she'd like for you to find someone to make you happy." He leaned over and kissed her cheek. He'd like to be that man. "Maybe you should make me a gooseberry pie."

She laughed. "That would be a good way to run you off. Besides, the gooseberries are gone for this year—blackberries, too." Abruptly, she sprang to her feet, a new light in her eyes. "But the persimmons are ripe. Let's go see." She held out her hand to pull him up.

He took her hand, the urge to pull her down on top of him strong. Instead, he pushed off the tree to give her leverage.

She tugged him along into the woods as the setting sun threw the forest into dark shadows. "We don't want to get lost in here," Ben reminded her.

"We won't. I know these woods as well as my own apartment." Rebecca stopped and surveyed the area as if taking her bearings. "There are some nice wild persimmons around here, and they taste so much better than those at the grocery store." Hooking his arm, she broke into a run.

Ben had never seen a persimmon tree before, and these were taller than he expected, but there weren't many left hanging on the trees. "Looks like we're too late. They've all fallen off."

"The fruit isn't sweet enough until it falls off, and the wildlife already had their fill. They've left a lot on the ground."

Most of the fruit appeared to be rotted, but Ben fell on his knees along with Rebecca to pick over those still edible. "Can you make a pie out of persimmons?"

She looked up from under her lashes. "Not even if I could make pie. No way to remove the seeds." She popped one in her mouth. "You have to use your teeth and tongue to get the flesh off," she mumbled, demonstrating, then spit out the seeds. "Like that. Hold out the tail of your tee-shirt so I can take some. We'll have to give some to Jamie."

"Jamie has really taken to you. I think he loves you as much as I do." He didn't realize what he'd said until she gave him a startled look, her features turning serious.

She reached out and used his shoulder for support as she rose to her feet. "I love both of you, too."

Dusk closed in more rapidly than Ben had noticed. "We have plenty of persimmons. Better get going now."

"No, let's go back to the oak. Your jeep is within sight, even in the moonlight. I don't want the day to end."

"All right." Holding the cache of persimmons secure with his left hand, he took Rebecca's with the right. Back at the tree, he dumped the fruit in the burger bag and settled down beside her.

She stared at the sky. The pale, crescent moon hung directly above them, surrounded by a million twinkling stars. "I love the city lights at night, but they can't compare with that view."

Maybe it was that moment Ben realized he loved her, not just as a friend. He understood her spirit better than anyone he'd ever known, even Kelly. And Rebecca had changed him—made him want to dream again.

"What was the miracle that happened out here?"

She kept her gaze fastened on the sky and instead of answering, asked a question of her own. "Do you know why Jamie and I get along so well?"

He thought he did. She was a loveable person, and more importantly, seemed to enjoy spending time with Jamie. As a matter of fact, that was one of the reasons he'd fallen in love with her. "Why?"

"Locking me in the shed with the spiders wasn't the worst thing my father ever did to me." She pulled up the sleeve of her sweater and turned her forearm to him. Even in the pale light, the marks were plainly visible. Scars caused by round burns, exactly like those on Jamie's arms. Distinctive. Cigarette burns.

"This was the only place I remember where my father was pleased with me. The only place where all three of us were happy. Maybe I pleased him only because I'd find grubs for his fish bait, but it was enough then."

Ben took her into his arms and kissed the top of her head, then slipped his mouth close to her ear. "I'm so sorry, Rebecca. You're the strongest survivor I've ever known."

She snuggled onto his chest. "In retrospect, I can

see how all things work together for good. Because I wanted to leave home so badly, I studied ten times as much as I had to so I could graduate early and get a scholarship to college. And I managed to finish high school at fifteen and get accepted to Emory. In a way I owe that to my father."

"Where was your mother in all this?" He knew how hard it was for a woman to break away from an abusive husband.

"She did her best. He never treated her badly, and she truly loved him. She could usually protect me."

"When did he die?"

She looked up at him and furrowed her brows like she had to figure up the time. "It's been close to ten years now. I can hardly believe it." She settled back into the crook of his arm. "I was in my junior year in undergraduate study when he called and ask me to meet him out here. The pain was still so fresh I almost declined, but I guess curiosity made me come.

"I'm glad I did. He told me he was dying from liver cirrhosis and asked for my forgiveness."

"That's the miracle? That he repented and asked for forgiveness."

"No, the miracle was I *could* forgive him." She got to her feet. "We'd better go now."

They said little on the ride back into the city, each lost in thought. Ben dropped her at her apartment building and had just cleared the heavy traffic on his way home when his phone rang.

Even though he'd had the jeep equipped with a

phone holder, he wouldn't normally answer while driving, but Rebecca's name flashed on the screen. "Hi, hon, what's up?"

Rebecca's frantic voice rose with each word. "Mrs. Gilly was knocked out. There's blood on the back of her head. I don't know how long—"

"Hold on. Who's Mrs. Gilly?"

"My cleaning lady. No telling how long she's been lying here, but she's still alive. I called 911 and the ambulance is on the way."

Ben was already looking for an exit. "Okay. I'm turning around. Call Darcy. You need someone with you until the ambulance gets there." He prayed Darcy would be at home. "Did you tell them to send the police?"

"I did. Just hurry."

"I am. I'm hanging up now so I can find a turn. Call Darcy."

He found one of those connectors cut across the interstate dividers by law enforcement to make a fast U-turn. It wasn't a proper exit, but he didn't see any cop cars stationed along the road.

While waiting for the traffic to clear, he called Tom, asking him to meet at Rebecca's apartment. No time to explain as he had to pull out in the north lane. His pulse and car accelerated at the same speed. He couldn't leave Rebecca alone tonight, even if he had to camp outside her door.

Then as he hit the perimeter, traffic slowed to a crawl. All sorts of possibilities flew through his mind as he sat fuming in the bumper-to-bumper traffic.

Had Jason been lying in wait in Rebecca's apartment and slugged the cleaning woman when she came in? Or was it someone from Bay Phar? But how would they have gotten in?

He hoped and prayed Tom could figure it out—and fast.

Chapter 15

And I say to you My friends, do not be afraid of those who kill the body, and after that have no more that they can do. -Luke 12:4

I've often wondered how I would react if faced with certain death. Now I know. -Rebecca Atkins.

Rebecca read the police report for the third time, and it revealed nothing more than what she already knew. Mrs. Gilly remained in a coma, her assailant unknown. Security cameras had caught nothing suspicious. No one had seen anything amiss.

Whoever attacked the cleaning lady had to have been hiding in wait, since the nature of her injuries indicated she didn't know what hit her. That meant he had to have entered the apartment sometime after four o'clock Saturday afternoon, because that's when Rebecca had left with Ben. That wonderful picnic by Lake Haven seemed so long ago, she wondered if she'd dreamed it.

At least a dozen people had asked her if she had locked the door when she left. She was certain she had.

Ben's concern touched her soul. He'd wanted to stay with her. She'd convinced him that wasn't necessary, that she'd spend the night with Darcy. But he'd insisted on coming to take them to church the next morning, although that meant he'd have to drive into the city, far out of his way.

Today she'd taken off from work for the first time in she couldn't remember when, but she and Ben had gone to the police precinct for an interview with the detectives. Truthfully, she put more faith in Tom Laster who was continuing his investigation. Her phone sounded the familiar jingle.

Ben.

His name flashing on the screen had a way of lifting her spirits and putting a smile on her face. "Hello, sweetie."

"You're sounding better. Where are you?"

"In my apartment. Security is on."

"Good. I'm taking you out to your favorite restaurant. Tom's coming with us. He has some new information. I'll pick you up right after work."

She noted the time. "That's an hour. I'd better start getting ready. I want to look good for you."

"You always look good to me."

"Ah, you're sweet, but I'm going to freshen up, anyway. See you in a few."

She laid out her navy sweater tunic, the one with the big pockets, and cream-colored pants. Her shower took less than ten minutes. Since the spider incident, she didn't spend long in the shower.

After a light application of make-up, she was considering what to do with her hair when the doorbell rang. That couldn't be Ben already, but who else could it be?

She brought up her security app. Derek Gammon stood outside her door. Activating the microphone, she asked, "Can I help you?"

"Yes, Ms. Atkins. I don't know if you remember me from Bay's."

"I do. You're in Bio Research."

"That's right. My brother is Tad Smalley, head of maintenance for this building. Actually, my half-brother. I'm purchasing an apartment here, and he said you got Southern Charm Decorators to furnish your apartment. I was wondering if I could come in and see their work."

"I'm sorry, but I have an appointment in fifteen minutes and I'm getting ready."

"I understand it's inconvenient, but I wouldn't take

up more than a minute of your time."

"Hold on while I check." She dialed Maintenance. "Is this Tad Smalley?"

"Yes, how can I help you?"

"Mr. Gammon is here—says he's your brother and you told him about my decorators."

"That's right. I remember how much you liked how they did your apartment."

"Just checking. Thank you."

She opened the door. Gammon nodded with a friendly smile. He wore a turtleneck and a knitted hat. "Is it that cold outside?" She stood back for him to enter.

He laughed, removing the hat. "It is pretty chilly. As I said, I won't be but a minute." He swiveled his head in a sweeping gaze. "I'll start with the living area. I love the open concept."

"Yeah, I do, too. They called the decorating style shabby chic. Most of the apartments are done in modern or industrial loft, but I found those cold for my taste."

"I'm not fond of that, either." He strode around the island.

Rebecca turned around to the wall of cabinets. The only thing cluttering the shiny granite countertop was a peach, left over from a cobbler Darcy had made. It probably came from Florida or South America, the Georgia peach season being well past. Darcy said imported peaches weren't good for anything but cobblers.

Rebecca dropped the peach in her pocket. She'd give it to Ben to take to Jamie. "I would offer you some refreshments, Mr. Gammon, but my boyfriend will be here to pick me up in a little bit." No harm in reminding him. She observed her reflection in the microwave's glass door.

"I'm afraid not, Ms. Atkins. You're coming with me."

"What?" She swirled around and recoiled at the Glock 38 pointed at her. "What are you doing?"

"Just getting rid of an obstacle. Trouble is, I haven't worked out the fine details yet, so I'm taking you to my house for holding."

Rebecca had once lost control of her car going around a curve. A strange calm came over her then—supernatural really—as the vehicle wove from one side of the two-lane road to the other. When the speed dropped, she regained control just in time to avoid an eighteen-wheeler coming in the opposite direction.

That same calm draped its arms around her now. "Why?"

"When my good friend, Lyle Moran told me how inferior you were for the chief of research position—remember, the position you stole from me—I decided I'd had enough of political correctness taking what's rightly mine. Then he told me how you convinced Dr. Breckenridge to choose you—" His laugh belied the sneer on his face. "I knew the only way to correct the situation would be to simply rid the world of women like you."

He was insane as well as pure evil. "Could I go to the bathroom first? I feel sick. You don't want me to mess up your car."

"All right, but don't try anything or try to leave a message. I inspected every inch of your bathroom when I left the spiders in there."

It took all her effort to turn her back on that gun as she moved quickly to the bathroom.

"And hurry up. If your boyfriend gets here before we leave, I'll have to kill him."

She left the door cracked so he'd know she hadn't locked it—and so he could hear her retching sounds.

Frantically looking for a weapon, she turned on the water. Nothing sharper than a pair of tweezers appeared. She turned the water off and pretended to retch again.

She could write a note with the eyebrow pencil, but there was nothing to write on. Dropping a washcloth in the sink she turned the water back on and shoved the tweezers in her pocket. Her hand came in contact with the peach.

Shutting off the water, she wrung the washcloth out and sat on the toilet, peach and tweezers in hands, and considered what to carve into the flesh of the peach.

The word help was useless. Anyone finding her missing would know she needed help. No—Gammon's name. Better still, his address. He said he was taking her to his house. And she knew he lived on Peachtree Street. She remembered it from searching his personnel data.

She searched the recesses of her brain for the address. In school, she'd had a photographic memory. Squeezing her eyes shut, she let the question float in her mind. Nine-four-something. A three-digit number for sure. She was pretty sure the last number was a seven.

As if of their own accord, her hand used the sharp edge of a tweezer to carve the numbers, then the P and the E. As she started the A, the door burst open. Fortunately, the toilet was almost hidden from the entrance, giving her enough time to drop the peach and tweezers in her pocket.

She jerked the wet washcloth up as if just removing it from her face.

"What are you doing? Get out of there. We're leaving."

She slid by him and his gun. He glanced back in the bathroom as if making sure she hadn't scrawled a message.

"Where are your car keys?"

"In my handbag." The bag sat on the corner counter, and she started for it.

"Stay. I'll get it." Not taking his glare off her, he reached his hand into her bag and scrounged until he found the keyring and pulled it out. He threw them to her. "You'll be driving."

"You're taking my car?" That hadn't occurred to her. What if Ben thought she'd gone somewhere?

"I took the Marta here. We can hardly leave that way." He pulled the sweater's collar up over his mouth and the hat low on his brow, then gestured with the gun for her to go to the door.

He followed close behind and reached around her to open the door. In that moment when his head was turned to the door, she grabbed the peach and tossed it behind her.

She prayed it would land in a place clearly visible to the first person entering the apartment. And that Gammon wouldn't look back.

Chapter 16

He delivers and rescues, and He works signs and wonders in heaven and on earth Who has delivered Daniel from the power of the lions. -Daniel 6:27

I have to believe the same One Who rescued Daniel from the lions' den can rescue my love. - Ben Lucas

While Ben negotiated the traffic from Tom's house, the detective examined his notes. He would be probing Rebecca's work associates tonight, and Ben wasn't surprised when Tom asked, "Rebecca said some of the people at work were hostile when she first arrived at Bay, but were coming around. Did you know her when she first took the position?"

"No. Even though we work in the same building, I met her at church. She's the Singles Sunday School director. In any event, she'd only been at Bay in the chief of research position about a month. She told you about the guy who held that position before her."

"Lyle Moran. I've compiled a profile of all the suspects. Moran doesn't fit the profile of a guy who goes postal."

"What?"

"Back in the nineteen-eighties a postal employee shot and killed fourteen fellow workers. From that incident we get the term 'going postal' to describe workplace rage."

"I know what 'going postal' means. Why wouldn't he fit? He had to blame Rebecca for taking his job. He already had a low opinion of women in general, didn't he?"

"I don't think so. I interviewed his wife. She didn't come across as a dominated woman. Besides, she said Moran is happier in his new position. On top of that, he was treated well by the company—given another job and allowed to retain his salary."

"What about the ex-boyfriend, Jason?"

"Jason Jackson. He's enough of an egotist to fit the profile of an ex who won't accept rejection. But he's more the playboy than stalker. I still have him on my radar, though."

His phone fitted on his dash rang and Rebecca's name flashed. "Hello, honey. We're on our way but the traffic's heavy."

"Take me off speaker." Rebecca's voice was clipped. Tense.

He did as she asked and shoved the earbud connected to the phone in his right ear. "What's up?"

"I think I have a stomach virus or something like that. I'm not going to be able to go out to dinner. Sorry. Please ask Tom for a raincheck."

"Is there anything I can get you?"

"No, Darcy's coming. I'll be all right in the morning. Tell Jamie I love him. I'll call you when I get to work."

"Yeah, sure. If you're able to get to work. I'll stop by in the morning to check. Both Jamie and I love you."

A long pause followed. "Okay, that'll be fine. See you then. Don't worry about me. Good-bye."

"What was that all about?" Tom asked.

Ben told him. "I don't like the way she sounded. If you don't mind, I want to swing by her apartment before we eat."

"Good idea."

Ben pulled into the parking garage and found the two slots assigned to Rebecca's apartment.

Both were empty. He gave Tom a started glance. "Her car's missing."

"You said she called saying she was sick. Maybe she had to go to the ER."

That thought didn't do much to slow Ben's racing pulse as he called Rebecca's number, leaving it on speaker. It rang ten times.

"We are sorry. That number has been disconnected."

"Don't jump to conclusions," Tom said. "Sometimes that message comes on when the battery runs down."

Ben opened the car door. "I'm going up."

"Right behind you."

The crowded elevator seemed to take forever to reach the seventeenth floor, stopping on every floor. Ben and Tom were the only occupants when the doors opened at the seventeenth.

They jogged down the hall. At Rebecca's door, Ben pounded with his fist while Tom rang the doorbell. "Rebecca, open up," Ben shouted loud enough for the neighboring residents to hear.

Tom reached around him and grabbed the doorknob. It turned. He pushed it open, and Ben would have plowed after him, but Tom held him back. "Better let just me go in. The police won't want anything disturbed. Why don't you go down and get Darcy? She might know something."

"I'll call her." Ben wasn't budging from this place. Likely Tom didn't want him to go in because he hoped to save his friend from finding Rebecca's bloody, lifeless body.

Darcy hadn't heard from Rebecca all day. She knew nothing about her being sick. By the time Darcy rang off, Tom came back out and closed the door behind him. "No one in there now. Nothing looks disturbed." He held something in his hand.

"What's that?"

Tom showed him.

A peach? "This was lying on the floor, the only thing out of place. I called the police."

"I thought you said the police wouldn't want anything disturbed."

"This may be a clue they'd ignore." He turned it around. "Someone carved these numbers and letters on it. Was Rebecca in the habit of doodling on her fruit?"

Ben grabbed the peach. "Of course not. Looks like nine-four-seven-P-E-I. What does it mean?"

The sound of running feet had both of them turning in that direction. Darcy came to a breathless halt. "What's happened? Where is Rebecca?"

"Looks like she may have been abducted. Do you know anything about this peach?" Ben shoved it at her.

She looked from one man to the other. "It looks like one of the peaches I used to make peach cobbler the other night. What of it?"

"Do you have any idea why Rebecca might have carved these particular numbers and letters on it?"

Darcy squinted, staring at the peach. "Has she ever done anything like that before? Has she ever mentioned writing messages on fruit?" Tom asked.

"No, not that I know of." Darcy's brows suddenly

shot up and her jaw dropped. "Oh, yes. We were watching old movies one night last week. We have a standing movie night on Thursdays. I was working on my wedding list so I wasn't paying much attention, but Rebecca was really into it. Some old movie about a woman who was kidnapped and scratched a note on her watch and put it around a cat's neck. They found the crooks by following the cat. I remember Rebecca remarking how clever that was. I agreed it was original."

"I remember that movie," Tom said. "Some teen flick. The surfer kids got involved when the FBI discounted their theory."

"How does that help us here? We don't have a cat to follow."

"We'll have to google every street in Atlanta that begins with PEI." Tom said it like anyone would know that. "And maybe the police will help us. They can check the security cameras and put out an APB on Rebecca's car."

"If they ever get here." Ben held the peach up to eye level, trying to discern if he'd overlooked anything. "Wait. I know the street. Peachtree. This third letter isn't an I. See how it's slanted. It's one side of an A. She must have gotten interrupted and dropped it to the floor."

Tom nodded and Darcy said, "It's possible."

"Let's go. Darcy can wait for the police and tell them what happened. While I'm driving you can check your profiles and see if anyone lives at this address."

"Do you know how many streets there are in Atlanta that have Peach in the name?"

"How many?"

"Seventy-one."

"Atlanta is proud of their Peachtree Street, I guess," Darcy said.

Tension had the nerves in Ben's temples throbbing. "We'll search all seventy-one then. Seconds count after an abduction. You know the longer it takes to find someone taken, the less chance of finding them alive. You check the details while I drive."

"Darcy, lock up here and wait for the police down stairs. Call and let us know how things are going." Tom turned to Ben. "Let's roll."

It took Ben half an hour of grueling traffic before Tom indicated the first turn. "While you look for the address, I'll be checking the addresses of our suspects," he said. "Oh, by the way, be on the look-out for Rebecca's car." Tom had already called his office and had them checking the address of every employee at Bay Phar. They were to call him back if they found any with a Peachtree Street address.

Ben itched to tear down the open road, but the thirty-mile-an-hour limit held him back. He couldn't afford to be stopped by a traffic cop. Besides, they had to check every square inch, something that became increasingly hard as full dark fell. Some of the streets didn't have street lights.

He kept his high-beams on, much to the annoyance of oncoming traffic.

The phone rang. Tom's office. He grabbed it out of its holder as fast as a six-gun out of the holster. All Ben could hear was, "Uh-huh. Uh-huh. Uh-huh. Got it." He hung up.

"Francine Eagleton, Lenard Samms, and Derek Gammon. You remember Rebecca mentioning any of those names?"

"No. Call Darcy."

Tom put the phone back on speaker, and Darcy's southern drawl came through, "Hello."

"Are the police still there?"

"Yes. I told them what you said, and they're still up there. They wouldn't let me in, so I've been checking with the security guy. He showed me the camera and it caught the guy taking Rebecca all right, but he had a turtleneck pulled up and a knit hat pulled down so you couldn't tell anything."

"Right. I'm going to give you three names. Tell me if you recall hearing Rebecca mention any one of them. Francine Eagleton?"

A long pause before Darcy said, "No, and I think that's a name I would have remembered."

"Lenard Samms?"

"No, that doesn't ring a bell at all, and I would have remembered since I'm engaged to a Sam."

"Derek Gammon?"

Another long pause. "That one sounds familiar. Yes, I think she's mentioned it, but I probably wasn't paying attention, but I think he was somebody from where she works."

"When the police come down, tell them to send reinforcements to Gammon's address." Tom referred to his notes, then gave her the address.

"That's a different number than on the peach," Ben said.

"She was off by one digit. Turn around. It's five streets back."

Ben made a U-turn right in the middle of the street and, regardless of traffic cops, turned the emergency lights on and sped up.

He took a left into a quiet, hilly, affluent neighborhood of mostly two-story brick colonials with walk-out basements. Ben clenched the steering wheel, ready for anything and praying harder than he ever had in his life.

"Cut the lights," Tom said. "Park on the street on the left side. Leave the cops plenty of room."

And so they wouldn't be noticed by the house's occupants. Lights shone in windows on both floors.

"Here." Tom shoved a handgun at him. "And stay behind me." They got out and quietly shut the doors behind them.

Crouching down, they scampered along the edge of the yard, avoiding the outside lights and, hopefully, the security systems. Ben grabbed Tom's shoulder. "Look." His raspy whisper barely disturbed the silence. "Rebecca's car."

Her navy sedan, hidden in the brush between an outbuilding and the neighbor's property. Tom nodded. "Let's go to the front door, just follow my lead. Keep your weapon in your pocket but with your hand on it. We don't know who's in there with Gammon."

Both men stood and walked with purpose toward the house. Ben hoped they could take Gammon before the police got here. If not, he might barricade himself with Rebecca in there.

Tom rang the doorbell. Once. Twice. It wasn't yet nine. Surely the people hadn't gone to bed yet—not with all the lights on. On the third try, the door opened a slit. "Yes, who is it?"

"I'm a neighbor from down the street, Charles Dawson. My car overheated. It's an older model." He laughed. "I can't get ahold of my wife, and I was hoping you could give me some water. That would cool it enough for me to get home."

Ben prayed Gammon would buy the lie as the seconds ticked off.

The door widened. "Of course, come in."

They stepped into a spacious living, dining, kitchen area with no sign of another occupant. "This is my friend, Dan Jordan. We've been on a hunting trip in my old jeep."

"Fine." Gammon's voice was clipped. "I have an empty milk jug to put your water in. Wait here. My wife isn't feeling well."

"Sorry to have disturbed you." Tom kept following. "As we were coming up your yard, Dan noticed the car parked beside your house that looked like a friend of his. Do you or your wife know Rebecca Atkins?"

Gammon froze in his tracks, but he didn't bother to

turn around. "No, I know nothing about such a person."

"You don't? She works in the same company as you."

"I think you're mistaken." Gammon suddenly swung around, gun raised and fired.

Chapter 17

And the peace of God, which surpasses all understanding, will guard your hearts and minds through Christ Jesus. -Philippians 4:7

I truly don't understand this calm—this peace—but I know Who sent it. -Rebecca Atkins

Bound and anchored to a support post in the dark basement, Rebecca jumped at the noise of gunfire. Two shots, then the sound of running feet. Then silence.

She'd been held for hours, though it had seemed

like days. As soon as they'd arrived at Gammon's house, he'd dragged her down the stairs and tied her, hands and feet, to this post. "Enjoy your night down here," he said, ignoring her questions and pleas. At the stairs, he'd turned, and she saw madness darting from his eyes.

"You won't be alone, Miss Atkins. This is where I keep my spiders, and they come out in the dark."

He'd cut the light and the click of the closing door was the last thing she'd heard until the gunshots.

That aura of peace remained with her—something she couldn't begin to understand. Even the thought of a night with spiders crawling over her didn't strike her with fear. Her rational brain told her spiders—no spider—would bite unless disturbed. Their prey was insects, not humans.

Even more astonishing, she felt the Holy Spirit with her, reassuring her that all would be well. And it would, regardless of the outcome. Whether she lived or died. She didn't have to worry about Ben and Jamie, her parents or her friends. A loving God was watching over all of them.

This uncanny feeling was so amazing, she'd lain here, propped against the post, basking in the wonder of it all.

The swoosh of the door at the top of the stairs pulled her attention in that direction. Then light blinded her for the moment. Her heart swelled and threatened to beat out of her chest as the moment of truth arrived. Would she be going home to be with the Lord or would she be going home with Ben?

"Ben." She sensed his presence even before seeing his handsome form. No matter how long she lived, this moment of him rushing to her would be burned into her memory as one of the most joyful of her life.

"Rebecca—thank God you're okay." He pulled a knife and cut the ropes holding her. Then took her in his arms.

Now that she was safe, she lost it. Sobbing. Shaking. Holding on tight.

"You are all right? He didn't hurt you...in any way." There was tension in the question.

She nodded against his chest. "I'm all right now. No, I'm unharmed. I knew you'd come. Somehow I knew."

"We found your peach."

"I didn't have time to finish the address."

"Between me and Tom and Darcy, we figured it out. I just knew I wasn't about to wait for the police to look for you. I know they do their best, but they don't love you like I do."

"And I love you with all my heart. My only real fear was not seeing you again."

He cradled her face in his hands. "If you love me, will you promise me something?"

She hiccupped, expecting him to ask that she take threats more seriously. "I owe you my life. Anything you ask."

"Will you marry me? Be my wife and Jamie's mother." He laughed shortly. "I don't suppose you ever expected to receive a marriage proposal in a mad scientist's basement."

"I'll take it anyway. Yes, I'll be honored to be your wife and Jamie's mother."

Siren sounds announced the arrival of the police. "What happened out there?" she asked. "I heard shots. Is Gammon dead?"

"I don't think so. Tom hit him, but he'll probably live to stand trial."

"Was Tom hurt?"

"No, he's good at dodging bullets, especially from a man who doesn't know how to shoot."

Ben scooped her in his arms. "The police can wait until tomorrow to question you. I'm going to insist you go home." He started for the stairs, holding her in his arms like she was a treasure of great worth.

"I can walk."

"I know, but I like the feel of you."

"Wait a minute." She put her arms around his neck and they kissed. Deeply, tenderly, with a promise of much more to come.

Epilogue

Eight Months Later

My beloved spoke, and said to me, "Rise up, my love, my fair one and come away. For lo, the winter is past. The rain is over and gone. The flowers appear on the earth. The time of singing has come, and the voice of the turtledove is heard in our land." -Song of Solomon 2:10-12

I never believed my heart could hold this much love. -Rebecca Atkins

"Girl, you're going make Ben forget his lines." Darcy

finished anchoring Rebecca's veil and stood back. Darcy was her matron of honor.

"He'd better not. I'm not leaving this church until I'm married...to him."

Janice Marshal, one of her bridesmaids, stuck her head through the door of the room off the church's vestibule. "Look who's here."

Rebecca turned from the mirror. "Mama." She tripped over her train as she covered the short distance to her mother. "You made it after all," she said, coming out of the hug.

"Yes, Carl pulled some strings and we got an earlier flight. I couldn't miss my baby's wedding, could I?" Rebecca's parents had been on a European vacation and their plane had been delayed in London.

"So, Carl can walk me down the aisle?"

"He's right outside, looking oh so handsome, beaming from ear to ear." Her mother hugged her again. "Speaking of handsome. I met your Ben. I already feel like he's the son I never had. I'm so happy for both of you, and I can't wait to spoil little Jamie."

"I bet you will."

The attendants were trying to free Rebecca's train so Mama stepped back. "I'll be forever grateful to Ben for rescuing my baby from that horrible man. He's been locked up for good, I hope. Have they had the trial yet?"

"There won't be a trial. Derek Gammon hung himself in jail right before the trial was to take place."

Mama pressed a hand to her mouth. "I can't say I'm

sorry. At least you'll be spared that. What about that poor woman he sent to the hospital?"

"She made a complete recovery, though she was in the hospital four months."

"Well, thank goodness, she'll be spared a trial too."

"It's still sad," Rebecca said. "When he was tying me up down in his basement, I tried to witness redemption to him. You know, like that woman who was kidnapped talked her kidnapper into releasing her by telling him about God's love. But it just made Gammon angrier. I'm afraid it's like the Bible says, that some are given over to a reprobate's heart and can't be reached."

"It can't be understood," Darcy said. "Why would he have singled you out in the first place?"

Rebecca shrugged. "Who can know? Jealousy, hatred, pure evil—maybe insanity."

Janice hooked Mama's arm as the strains of the prelude to the wedding march sounded. "Time to take your seat." She looked back over her shoulder. "And time for you to get in position," Janice said to Rebecca. "The next time you walk that aisle, you'll be an old married lady."

Darcy giggled. "Like me." Darcy and Sam had married that Christmas and purchased a house a block down the street from Ben's house in Haven. She hadn't regretted swapping the glitz of the city for the quiet of the suburbs at all. And neither would Rebecca.

She marched down the aisle on the arm of her step-father on one side and little Jamie on the other in a ceremony of gasps, smiles, tears, and sheer joy, sealed in a kiss.

In the middle of the reception, she stole down the back stairs and beckoned to Ben, who waited for her cue. With Tom's help they made their get-away. Everyone except Tom and Darcy thought the couple would be off on their Caribbean honeymoon. They wouldn't know until later about this detour.

"I feel guilty not telling Jamie good-bye," Rebecca said as Ben pulled the twenty-four-foot camper onto the highway.

He leaned over to sneak a kiss. "We'll make it up to him later. Besides, our parents will be so busy spoiling him, he won't even miss us."

The dirt road to Lake Haven wasn't far, and they soon parked at the familiar picnic sight.

They walked hand-in-hand to the sandy shore to enjoy the sunset. "The next few days belong to just us, honey." Ben pulled her close. "Just you and me and God and the little woodland creatures."

That's the way it felt to her, too, and it was a wonderful feeling.

In the darkness of the forest, fireflies pulsed in rhythm with the stars overhead and the sweet smell of honeysuckle wafted on the soft summer breeze. Rebecca lifted her face, seeking his kiss. Ready for their love to be melded. At one with nature. At one with each other. At one with God where there is no beginning and no end.

Author's Note

Thank you, dear reader, for reading *A Pursued Heart*, Book 2 in the *Georgia Peaches* series.

Readers are so important to the success and growth of good Christian fiction. If you enjoyed this book, please help us promote it by letting your friends know through social media and word of mouth. Subscribe to my newsletter and receive a free ebook, *Cloaked in Love*, and announcements about future books.
https://dl.bookfunnel.com/or10xrsvje

And, most important, pray for me and other authors. The publishing industry is an important way to enlighten the public about the love of God in an entertaining way. Since reviews are more important than ever for books to get noticed, please leave a review at Amazon and Goodreads. I write only for the Lord's glory and the reader's pleasure, so I would much appreciate your opinion.

Coming Next in this Series

Search for Contentment by Marlene Bierworth

Melanie Braxton is a police officer in South Carolina fighting for freedom from her family's affluence. Trevor Knight is a lawyer, struggling to keep what remains of his family together.

Trevor and Melanie join forces to solve the mystery of his niece's death, while Cupid aims his arrow at their unsuspecting hearts.

See what happens when Melanie is forced to face her past to secure the future that she desperately wants. Faith and love are tested in this Christian, contemporary, mystery romance.

Other Books by Elaine Manders

The Annex Mail Order Brides series:

Adela's Prairie Suitor
Ramee's Fugitive Cowboy
Prudie's Mountain Man
The Annex Mail-Order Brides Boxset

Intrigue under Western Skies series:

Book 1, Pursued
Book 2, Surrendered
Book 3, Revealed
Book 4, Escaped

The Wolf Deceivers series:

Book 1, The Chieftain's Choice
Book 2, The Duke's Dilemma
Book 3, The Captain's Challenge

Westward Home and Hearts, a mult-author series:

Book 1, Lacy's Legacy
Book 3, Maggie's Christmas Miracle
Book 5, Bethany's Baby

Brides of Pelican Rapids, a mult-author series:

Elaine Manders

Book 5, Molly's New Song

Also:
The Perfect Gift, a Christmas Novella
The Washwoman's Christmas
Cloaked in Love

About the Author

Elaine Manders writes wholesome, Christian romance about the strong, capable women of history and present day and the men who love them. She lives in Central Georgia with a happy bichon-poodle mix. When not writing, she enjoys reading, sewing, crafts, and spending time with her daughter, grandchildren, and friends. You may contact the author at any of the following.

Facebook:
https://www.facebook.com/elaine.manders.35
Twitter: https://twitter.com/ehmanders
Email: elainehmanders@gmail.com
Bookbub:
https://www.bookbub.com/authors/elaine-manders
Goodreads:
https://www.goodreads.com/author/show/14151675.Elaine_Manders